INDIGO

Sky

By

Kay Carroll

Copyright Kay Carroll 2016

ISBN-10: 1534736190
ISBN-13: 978-1534736191

First Edition

All efforts were made to identify copyright holders. If an oversight was made, upon contact to the publisher the correction will be made in the next edition.

A dream forever deferred was never one to begin with…

@@@@

To mom… whose love lives on… and sweet memory continues to guide me.

Background

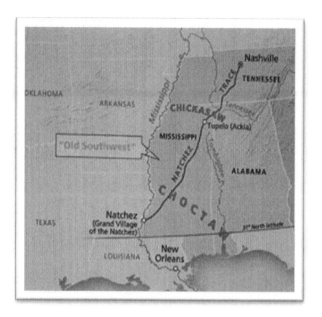

The Choctaw (In the Choctaw language, Chahta) are Native American people originally from the Southeastern United States (modern day Mississippi, Florida, Alabama, and Louisiana). The Choctaw language belongs to the Muskogean language family group. The Choctaw are descendants of the peoples of the Hopewell and Mississippian cultures, who lived

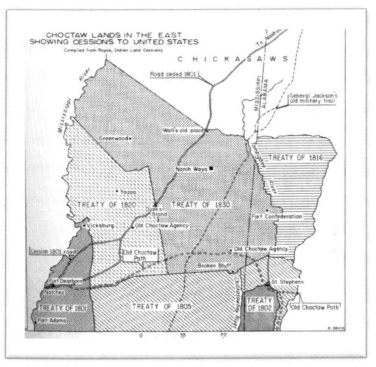

CHOCTAW LANDS IN THE EAST
SHOWING CESSIONS TO UNITED STATES
Compiled from Royce, Indian Land Cessions

throughout the east of the Mississippi River valley and its tributaries.

In the 19th century, the Choctaw became known as one of the "Five Civilized Tribes" because they adopted numerous practices of their United States neighbors. The Choctaw and the United States (US) agreed to nine treaties and, by the last three, the US gained vast land cessions and deracinated most Choctaw west of the Mississippi River to Indian Territory.

They were the first Native Americans forced under the Indian Removal Act. The Choctaw were exiled because the U.S. wanted to expand territory available for settlement by European Americans to save the tribe from extinction and to acquire their natural resources.

Grenada County, Mississippi– Setting: The Late 1800's

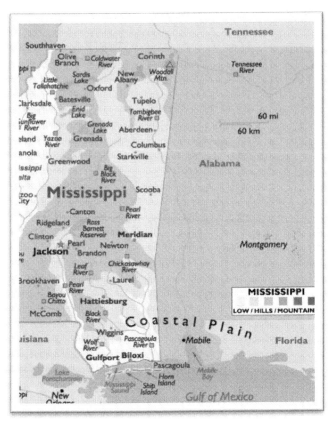

Mississippi -Late 1800's

From The Milcreek Pond Collection

Indigo Sky

"Hand it over, boy."

"I ain't got nothin' fo' you."

"He s-a-aid hand it over Jake, or he'll take off yo' head."

"But I ain't got nothing to give you, suh! What is it that you wont?"

Crack... Crack... Crack.

The distance between Corinth, Mississippi and Hardeman County, Tennessee is 42 miles. Corinth's location, at the junction of two railroads, made it strategically important to the Confederacy during the Civil War.

Mississippi has hilly areas, but no steep mountains. The highest point in Mississippi is 806 feet above sea level; locals call it Woodall Mountain. That's where they found him.

******

CH 1

(*M*)olly

March 1881- Grenada, Mississippi

When I first came back from Boston I was surprised that Ma did not meet me at the station herself, but sent our neighbor, who sharecropped on the land next to our plot. How he happened to be riding in Mr. Neuman's gray coach, I didn't know, but it was a rare sight to see a sharecropper in a contraption as fine as that one in Grenada, Mississippi. Mr. Neuman was a corn, soy, and wheat farmer and the only grain mill owner in the county. My entire family, Ma, Jake, and me, had worked for him and lived on the Neuman place in our quaint little stone-gray, three room shanty for as long as I could remember. I had never known Mr. Neuman to allow anyone besides himself, his manservant Ciaok, or my brother Jacob—whom everyone called Jake—to steer either of his coaches.

I got off the train and looked in every direction for either Ma or Jake; thinking then that my brother would have come back home from his trip up North. Instead, this wiry, bent over, slightly familiar frame stepped into my path.

"Your ma sent me 'long as she not be feeling her best," he said.

I bit my lower lip and squinted as I tried to recall the name attached to the pock-marked, unshaven face in front of me.

"Oh, yes...Stratt...Mr. Stratt, how are you? Thank you for coming for me, but where is Ma? You say she's not feeling well?"

I never knew Ma to take to her bed for anything, unless it was something serious—likened to yellow fever it would have to be.

"Well miss, it's been like this. Oh...akin to a year or so I reckon, since your brother, well...I don't have to tell you."

I wanted to shout, "Yes, you do have to tell me!" But, I wasn't about to ask this almost-stranger to tell me something about my mother and brother that he thought I should already know. So I nodded and held my tongue for a few moments to think this thing through before answering him, while he took all but one of my four bags and headed towards Mr. Neuman's tall black coach.

"Uh, no you don't have to tell me, Mr. Stratt, about Ma or Jake, that is." I finally said.

By the time the soft rawhide interior carriage was finally in view, I'd held my breath wondering when this quiet, somewhat mysterious fellow would speak again.

He turned around and looked at my face, drained of color, and must have realized that I didn't know as much as I pretended to.

"Miss," he said, "I'll start slow, but I 'thank you ought to know what had happened just last month."

We trekked back along and then across the railroad tracks, past the one-story frame Illinois Central depot. It was constructed only five years ago to serve both passenger and freight traffic. I looked across the way at the new hotels and businesses that were opening nearby on First Street, all the way to the public square.

I followed close to him, stepping up into the coach and handing him my last bag to place inside. I thought to get back out and climb up into the seat next to him on top to continue our talk—but decided not to. Before long he began sputtering, in his own dialect, loud enough for me to hear him from inside the warm, comfortable cabin while he steered the reins on top—spinning a tale which I still don't fully believe to this day.

"It was this a way here…I goes over to yo' shanty late one evening, that be on the fifth I 'thank, cause I know yo' ma, she be feeling down the last few months– well you knows why—and that's when I hears all this here hollering , sho' nuff ruckus going on in behind yo' place."

He paused as the rain came down, pelting his oversized dusty hat, drenching his face, and slowing our tracks. The rain slowed some while I waited for him to keep talking, but he didn't.

"And then?" I asked, anxiously.

"Well, I'm not sho' clear on what I saw then, even now. But I just tell you what I think I did see 'fore I got scared and run off, I'z shamed to say," he admitted, then stopped talking.

"Mr. Stratt, you were saying?"

" L'l 'Moe', I just don't want to say....don't know how...just leave it at yo' Ma ain't herself no mo'. It wuldn't be right, a sin even, fo' me to say mo', miss."

"Ugh," I hated that he pulled that nickname out of the past. I thought it was buried. Ole' Mr. Richmond at the mercantile in town started calling me by that name and I disliked it from the start. Especially when he first called me, 'Lil lap-legged Moe' which he shortened to 'Mo,' but I hated it just the same. Anyway, I'm healthy now, except for that last time, after the Autumn Festival when my left foot got heavy again and gave way. I think it was because I was so terrified, running through those dark woods from someone or something I couldn't see.

That didn't matter now, because I couldn't fathom his story here—knowing less than this stranger and probably everyone else in town about my own mother—so I pushed him to keep talking.

"But Mr. Stratt wouldn't it be more of a sin for you to burden me with those few frightening words about ma, than it would be if you were to tell me all you do know so that I can help her? Would you leave me to worry more than I already am?"

And about what, I didn't know.

We slowed down and then stopped. I slid across the leather seat, craning my neck and head out the window to find out why and found him staring in my direction.

After a moment, he commanded the horse to move on and then spoke to me, taking his time.

 "Well, I guess yuz right about that Miss Molly. I don't wont to cause you no extra grief."

I waited.

"So after I heard the ruckus, I tole you about, I turns and runs off, but I was so shamed that I went back 'gin and took my time moseying around the back. Then the hollering set off louder, so's I begins to run and stops and peeks 'round the side corner of the house, keepin' my body hidden best as I kin, and I see a body, sho' nuff believe it was yo' ma, but she didn't look like herself—caked-up dirt all over her. "

Now I was truly perplexed, remembering the "cleanliness next to godliness" inspections Ma faithfully administered to my brother Jake and me every week. Covered in mud? Not my Ma.

I was not sure I even wanted this man to go on now. I pictured the deep pockmarks on the side of his face, near his right ear, just below the down-turned weathered old hat. I felt my eyes become narrow slits—my signal for him to stop. Not able to see me, he just drove on and kept talking.

"But, it was her, alright," he said, "I'm sho'. She was on her knees next to your pump. Tha't somethin'…got yo' own water pump. Those Neuman's sho' was good to y'all. Not shore what happened why's they's changed….but…yas she was on her knees next to da pump, hollerin' like she was a banshee, never seen nothin' like it. Yo' woulda thought it was years 'go and she was been beat by her masta or overseer the way she was goin' on. Looked like she mayhap tried to wash some of the mess off, but she be covered with so much of it… some was crusted… like it been on her all day long. I then looks 'round to see if anyone was there with her—who did dis to her or hurt her like—but she was 'lone. I crept over towards her to see if I kin do something fo' her, but she hollered for me to git. I'd say she musta gotten into some "spirits" if it wuldn't yo' ma, and I doesn't mean spirits of the "udder world-like" either."

He finally stopped telling the tale, and the wind picked up slapping against the damp blowing leaves. Somehow I wasn't sitting in the coach anymore…not really. My mind had exited the window, away from him and his fantastic story. I could see the narrow, dirt path, through the avenue of spruce and pines toward the willow trees, near the waters. This was the only place I ever felt completely free. It was all that existed at the moment for me.

I heard myself speak.

"Not my Ma. I've never known her to drink or have anything to drink in the house, even while she worked at the Neuman's where drink was abundant and she could have as much as she could hold if she wanted."

Mr. Stratt had only sharecropped for about five years. We didn't know much about him and didn't care for what we knew. But there was no way to explain what he saw. I thought it best not to probe anymore about what he thought I already knew. If I did, it would only open my family to more unnecessary chatter from the townsfolk who had nothing better to do than gossip.

The peace that I felt when I stepped off the train had left me. A troubling feeling had set in. All I could think about was getting home to Ma. I prayed that Mr. Stratt was wrong about what he saw that day, but it didn't stop the images of my lovely, strong Ma with crazed eyes and filthy, writhing on the ground in pain. In about 30 minute's time, I would see Ma for myself—and the home that I left not two years ago. In an instant, memories of Boston and the charmed life that I led there seemed to vanish.

****

When I first left home and arrived in Boston, it was the autumn of 1879. My first northern winter, though, was memorable. The snow began just before Christmas. There was a chill in the air. And when the sun rose, it would glint off the fresh mounds of snow like a diamond in the light. I loved to hear it crunch beneath my feet. I spent two Christmases in Boston, chilled but blissful. I was living the life I'd always dreamed of—learning high society's lessons and gliding across the dance floor of glorious galas. When I wasn't perfecting my needlepoint skills, I was entertaining an array of suitors. But none of them had my heart—I wanted it to belong to John Wagner. By Dr. Wagner's third visit, I had grown smitten by this gentleman from Boston.

He was the doctor Aunt Minnie called when we arrived from Grenada on that chilly November afternoon, and I nursing a nagging cough which had lingered and turned into full-blown hacking.

I was lying in a pink ruffled dressing gown on yellow satin sheets relishing the flowery wallpaper and bright white-paned draperied windows when he strolled into the sunny bedroom. I squeezed my eyes shut, opened and shut them again, as he strolled towards the very edge of my feather bed. He was tall, at least six foot one with thick black hair, combed across a high, broad forehead and just above deep, dark brown eyes. His complexion was more of an olive coloring than anything else. I thought he had a kind of gypsy look about him.

"John… I mean… Doctor?"

When Dr. Wagner and I met for the first time, it was in Grenada, during the Yellow Fever plague, I was only twelve–too young to even notice John the man. He was also Mr. Neuman's nephew from Boston. The second time that I saw him was three years later when he came to Grenada's Autumn Festival.

The city he came from, Boston, had pockets of wealthy people. The Boston Brahmins, as they were known, were the upper crust—cultured, urbane and dignified. Life there was dominated by something called politics that ran between them and Catholic immigrants. Boston was a transportation hub for that area called the New England region with its network of railroads. Even the everyday people in Boston considered their city, and those who lived there, to be more important and the best educated of all the northern folks. They had more hospitals—they called them medical medical centers—than I'd ever seen. And most people had more money too. Along with New York, Boston was the money capitol of the whole United States in that it especially important in funding railroads all over the country. Because of legislation, it was one of the few places in the North where Negro and white children could attend the same schools. It had also been the base for many anti-slavery activities. It was no wonder that I was so impressed with the people who happened to be born in such a place as this. I'd hoped that I might have run into my brother while I was in Boston. I thought that maybe he would have found work and a new life there.

Any man that came from this background had to be special. That's one reason I was so taken with John. The other was his extra gentle touch whenever he had to examine me. He touched my face, held my throat, and then clasped my hand to take my pulse, and it tingled wherever he touched.

I had a beau back home in Grenada whom I cared for—and was waiting for me—but this was different. Not that I'd given up on my beau, Alex, with his piercing dark eyes. He'd written to me regularly all the while I was away, but I believed a girl had to sun up her flowers while she's still young. Anyway, Alex was not even in Grenada to welcome me back home, but I forgave him because he had to go to Virginia to help his kin who needed him through harvest.

I liked to remember when Dr. Wagner and I met for the first time during the Yellow Fever plague, when I was only twelve. And when we danced three years later at Grenada's Autumn Festival. It was a fateful night. My dream had been marred that same evening when Mr. Neuman's place went up in flames and everyone in town blamed me. That night turned out to be embarrassing for us both. Dr. Wagner—because he'd admired and danced with "the accused" right up until I became the town spectacle.

Who would have believed I would run into Dr. John Wagner at Aunt Minnie's first of many "Welcome North" parties given in my honor. Aunt Minnie—

Mrs. Neuman's aunt really—became my "adopted" second mother. She rescued me from a life of drudgery and degradation in Grenada when she invited me to come and live with her in Boston. Aunt Minnie had her own rules. I first met her when she visited her niece, Mrs. Neuman, in Grenada before the Autumn Festival. Her husband Albert had passed away two years earlier. She felt her grieving period was over, and it was time to tackle life again. She believed the Autumn Festival would be just the thing to get her back to her old self.

I've heard the term 'stout' or 'bossy', when referring to Mrs. Millicent Granville—*my* Aunt Minnie. Others say she's an unpretentious, no-nonsense, older woman. But I just call her my fairy godmother...my kindred spirit.

I will never forget Aunt Minnie and her generosity or the princess treatment I received in a northern world that was so different from the one which I emerged. Since we first met in Grenada, in her pale-yellow, satin wallpapered guest bedroom with matching white chintz curtains, she's had me floating and fluttering around like a gazelle she named, "pretty one".

Although the memories are fading each day now that I'm back home, there are some particular moments I'm trying to hold on to...

For Aunt Minnie, Boston was her "Athens in America." She said it was "with her great pleasure" that she —this grand lady—introduce the city she loved to *me*. That included her close neighbors, friends, and shop merchants. Most of them were regulars on her guest lists. All my years of Ma's proper talking lessons in the front room of our little house came in handy when I attended Aunt Minnie's parties.

"Good Afternoon, yes, I'm Molly Elizabeth McCray. I'm so pleased to know you.

Oh, do I?

Yes, it's absolutely breathtaking...

I'm not a bit tired though.

I couldn't be happier to discuss the inner workings of your business, charity, or any anything else you deem important."

And on and on I'd go.

I remember reciting those singular lines with the determination of an actress whose career depended on perfect delivery. Once I started practicing the lines Ma gave me, I kept going until my tongue tired out and my throat parched.

We had entered the 1880s and I was living my dream in high style. My long, chestnut-brown plaits hung free to cascade in waves around my shoulders, laid bare in several custom-made long flowing dresses, gowns and two-piece outfits of every color. I'd even gained a natural rosiness to my cheeks to add to my peaches and cream complexion. But I had to admit, I didn't like the old men staring at me though; it felt creepy-crawly. If I saw their wives, I'd always try to head in their direction, which usually made their husbands stop. Throughout the room, most of ladies' dresses showed off stylish chemises with pointed necklines and lavishly trimmed collars. I would have expected more of a neckline, but Aunt Minnie said they thought it unhealthy and unvirtuous for women to expose their chests. Their blouses were layered, with full wrist-length sleeves. There were variations of about four different hairstyles, but most ladies in the room wore their hair up with bangs and some sort of bun on top, while a few had theirs cascading down the back of their neck. They all pranced throughout the room with fans and lace-trimmed parasols which they opened when they ventured outside through the double doors.

There were a few ladies who, instead of the two piece top and skirt, wore one, long, narrow dress. When I'd thumbed through *Godey's Lady's Book* on Aunt Minnie's cocktail table; those outfits were the newest thing on the front cover. From the neck to knee, the dress was straight. Below the knee, the skirt flared out and formed a shallow train. Some ladies at the parties, I'm shocked to say, had their knees tied together, making anything but small steps, much less dancing, impossible. They had moved the bustles on their outfits to a lower position than the ones on skirts. The colors of gowns were in darker green, red, and blue velvet, instead of the lighter airy yellows, whites, and pinks that were on display in *Godey's Lady's Book* for the spring and summer. Although my own two piece red and crème chiffon had a long billowy skirt, the more daring younger ladies wore skirts shortened to the ankle showing off their elegant shoes with high heels.

They arrived with small matching hats they left lying on the rack in the hall on their way through the parlor into the oversized, beautifully decorated entertaining room. I must have inhaled every brand of French perfume as the ladies drifted through the door—but even those expensive dabs couldn't mask unpleasant body odors. After each party ended, Aunt Minnie and I sat up in her room for hours talking about everything and everyone.

I thought the grandness of it all was more than I'd ever hoped to experience. Now here I am, Molly Elizabeth McCray going on 17, on my way home not two years later—and afraid of what may have happened while I was away.

CH 2

(M)

"For I know the plans I have for you," declares the Lord, "plans to prosper you and not harm you, plans to give you hope and a future." Since our Ma first spoke these words to us, my brother Jake and I had etched them in our minds.

They were also the words that came to mind when Ma met Mr. Stratt and I at the front door–looking twenty pounds lighter and ten years older than I remembered.

After a few weeks back now, I don't know if Ma or me feels the same anymore, 'cause we can't keep going with our lives until we can figure out what had happened.

So you'll understand, after what I've learned, why I haven't the strength to go on, but I'll try anyway.

During these weeks I've been back in Grenada, I thought I would forget Boston with all its happenings, but it turns out that all I can stand to think on is the past, because I can't bear the present as it now exists.

It took a couple of days for Ma to tell me the whole story after the puzzling Mr. Stratt dropped me off at home that Friday evening. It wasn't until then that Ma finally told me about how she'd gone up to Hardeman County, Tennessee, days before I'd left home. It was the day after I left for Boston with Aunt Minnie, the time I had to escape when the Autumn Festival ordeal had ruined my life, that Ma first began to fall apart.

I still can't understand why my beloved mother, whom I will forever refer to as "Ma", didn't stop me from leaving home or at least call me back from Boston when a stranger sent her a newspaper clipping of the death of a young man they believed to be my brother, Jake. When she got to Hardeman County, the officials said their smell-driven dogs followed Jake's scent from Tennessee through the Mississippi hills where they cut his body down from a tree. Ma said she questioned whether it was really her son she couldn't identify. Now no one seems to know where he is or what happened after he left home, thinking leaving would make him a man.

Ma said they showed her a body, shot full of holes, that they'd found hanging from a tree near the top of Woodall Mountain.

It didn't seem real. It wasn't like Jake to give anyone reason to want to hurt him. He always did what he was told, not like me. He didn't ask so many all-fired questions about why things were the way they were like folks said I did. He mostly said that he knew that life was the way it was, that he was grateful for the place he had on this farm, and he acted that way. We both knew Ma did her best, so Jake and I (in most things) did what we were told.

That autumn day, when Ma said she went up to Tennessee to identify the body, it's hard to understand why she couldn't tell if it was Jake or not. And now, almost two years later, she recounted the details of whom and what she'd seen when she arrived and was taken to that dank room.

I recognized her description of the speckled yellow shirt and newly stitched gray trousers Jake had brought home from ole' Mr. Richmond's store using money from his final pay from working at the mill the week before he left.

I remember spying them on Jake the day he came home with those new clothes, eased them from the store bag, and put them into a suitcase. When he caught me watching, he stopped me from shrieking. Jake was packing his traveling clothes.

As Ma described the torn, bloody clothes covering the body, I didn't flinch, but knew it was Jake alright. Ma never got to see the clothes on him while he was living. She told me she felt sure it wasn't him there lying dead on that pallet, but she couldn't tell for absolute sure. But after Ma said she had had no word from Jake since he left, I then realized the Jake we depended on would never leave for good, of his own free will, without a word to anyone.

Seeing Ma now. She had changed so much.

"Ma, you look tired."

She nodded gently, a few strands of hair falling away from her silver grayish temples.

"I am," she said.

"You know I would've come back sooner if you hadn't written me that falsehood saying that you'd heard from Jake that he was safe and had found work up North."

"That's what I didn't want," she said.

"Come again?"

Ma paused and pushed her long strands behind her left ear.

"...for you to come back."

She turned and looked at me. Then spoke slowly.

"You forget he didn't even know you went to Boston and that I was living here alone. He left before the Autumn Festival; we didn't plan on you going to Boston. But we knew that the fire at Mr. Neuman's caused you so much worry and you had to go away." she said.

Ma didn't need to remind me. The fire wasn't the only reason I wanted to leave. I'd always yearned for a bit of that other life and a feeling of total uninhibited freedom and imagined acceptance that I never received living in Grenada. At that time, it was all I ever wanted. I did not forget why I left home. And I had planned on staying away even longer, but Ma stopped writing.

Boston. I couldn't stop my thoughts from straying back...

Some things were just downright unbelievable. There was even something called indoor plumbing in their newfangled houses–connected to a water and sewer network. I found this out several moments after Aunt Minnie led me into the lilac colored sitting room that was to be mine while I was staying with her.

"This is so beautiful, and I don't... Aunt Minnie...um...I don't want to be a bother, but I don't see...

uh… a curtain or a chair with the open seat and porcelain pot under it like Mr. Neuman has back home. Will I go outside? Is there an outhouse in the back?" I asked.

Aunt Minnie certainly didn't laugh at me, but she almost did. She said at the time of the Civil War, only the wealthiest Bostonians could afford the luxury of indoor plumbing, but by the time I had arrived she had a toilet and running water inside and so did most everyone in the city. She even had a special room for the toilet and to take a bath in.

My figure had gotten a lot shapelier while I was away, too. I was noticeably self-conscious about it.

Now what am I doing thinking about Boston? But I had to do something to save my sanity. I'm gonna…*keep thinking on the past*…I told myself. Forget where I am at this moment, back in Grenada with Ma and no Jake.

During the month I was preparing to leave Boston to come back home, the cleaning lady who helped out at Aunt Minnie's and I became close. One afternoon she was in my room when I got in from a visit to one of the families I'd gotten to know so well. My chestnut hair was styled with slightly curled bangs over my forehead with the rest of my long wavy locks swept to the top of my head. When I took off my corset and was down to my drawers and stockings, she must have felt comfortable enough with me to comment on my blossoming appearance.

"Look at those hips, even without the corset." She said.

As one would expect, I would hear this from someone having no visible hips of her own to speak of. I figured her comments explained all the side glances from gentlemen when I tried out the new tight across-the-hips fashion that had just come out. Still, I was just plain embarrassed by her comment and had to say something.

"And would you look at those...," I responded to her. Then after a few seconds passed it was obvious I couldn't think of anything that made sense to finish up with–but, "of yours."

I stood there in my stockings and drawers pointing at her–she fully dressed–wearing a corset with no visible figure. I don't know what or how I meant my words to come out, but she could have taken it whichever way she wanted.

That was then. But I'm back home now, dragging along towards the small, gloomy corner room, where I sit down and wonder why am I back? There really is nothing for me here anymore. The same cold little dwelling place surrounded by the same white folks with the same hate-filled way of treating mulattos and Negros, as if we are not worthy of a moment's peace on this earth.

And there is Ma, in the next room talking to herself as though I had not left her side. I got up and walked back into the front room.

"But I was gonna write and tell him you were gone...yes, I was," she kept saying.

Looking at Ma... listening to her, I didn't know her. So in the days ahead, how was I going to help either of us? She was scaring me, and I wanted it to end. But instead of stopping, she held her stomach and bent over, the incessant talking now mingled with soft moaning.

"Ooooh…I made that trip to Tennessee…Lawd….
I saw that other boy… but I never saw my baaa-bee…
Oooh, they say it was my Jake, but I can't believe it…I
didn't know …I didn't know it was my baaa-bee… I
couldn't take it no mo'. I should've known by what he
had on….it was him alright!! Lawd….oooh my Lawd."

I held my hands in my lap to keep them from
covering my face. I needed to cry… to shake her; to
scream.

Then I asked her a question in my mind.

*How could you have known it was him by 'what he had on',
you say? Did you see those clothes in Jake's bag before he left that
day 'cause he wasn't wearing them when he left home and he never
showed them to you?!*

You didn't see them, Ma.

So you can't know!

You couldn't know!

But I knew; I had seen them.

In place of shouting confusing words and questions
at this fragile shell of my Ma, the tears streamed out the
corners of my eyes, down my cheek and onto my soft,
white bodice.

All I could do was cry. I hated everything. I hated
being back in Grenada. I hated that I'd ever left home
and gone to Boston. I should have been here, asking
what happened, easing Ma's pain.

Ma and I sat close in the dimly lit room. Outside of
the window, a long shadow moved and then blanketed
the pathway. The sun was fading into the distance. From
the front room, I could see its round orange glare between the mulberry branches. Ma was still rambling on
about Jake. She didn't seem to know I was even in the
room.

I thought about the cruelty of our situations, how unfair it was that something like this would happen and make someone as giving and kind as Ma turn out this way. I didn't even have time to grieve myself for my own brother.

What some vile vermin did to Jake circled my brain, leaving a red hot imprint. During Ma's ramblings, some things were made clear. As I listened closely, I learned that the Hardeman County sheriff found Jake only a month after he left home. Ma said someone there recognized his body and got word to her.

I clung to our cherished summer afternoons. Jake and I lounged around chatting during his lunch break at the mill. He would pull out an old wooden chair hidden behind a bush and I plopped down on the tree stump. We'd stare out at the lake. His lunch pail rattled from the all the pecans he packed inside like a squirrel.

"What is that?"

"What's what?" he quipped.

"That noise in your box…that's what?"

He smiled that long slow smile of his, saying nothing.

"Did you pack all those pecans in there again?" I demanded.

"Of course, what did you think it was?"

"Fine, but do you have to crack those things in the house? If I hear that crunch under my shoe one more time or have to pick up those hard husks and shell pieces from between the floor planks again like this morning, I'll hurt you——you stinkin', stankin' squirrel."

He picked a shelled nut out of his box and threw it at me. I caught it and placed it in my mouth and crunched on it.

"——'member when your feet used to stick out like this," he laughed, taking his feet and pulling his heels together at an angle to form a V shape.

He added, "Your hair all stuck to your head, matted-curly and bare feet sticking out sideways after swimming with your friends in Milcreek Pond."

"M mmm…'course I do. You don't have to remind me you stinkin' squirrel."

"For a spell you were plumb near waddling from side to side like a duck," he kept laughing.

"Uh-huh…you've had your put-on for today. So I walked like a duck–but I trained myself to walk the right way. Much better than you trying to talk proper. And why do you think everything is so darn funny?"

"I was just funning… you're forever making a mountain out of a molehill, girl," he said, turning away.

"That molehill would be a mountain to you too, if folks called you lap-legged every day," I said, putting down my sandwich that didn't taste as good anymore.

"Wouldn't bother me none," he said, lookingaround like he was searching for something.

"Oh… it would… you just wouldn't say nothin'."

"Aww, I was just funning that's all…," he said.

After that, we were both silent, watching wiry, high-strung kids throw handfuls of sticks and rocks back and forth across the sun-kissed waters.

It was on that one afternoon in particular I noticed a little White boy about six years old reaching out to help his scrawny, scared little swimming companion, who happened to be a Negro child, into the chilly waters.

"Look at them," I said to Jake.
He looked past me to the side of the shimmering blue lake to the two boys in the midst of the other young ones, taking turns, playing some kind of tag-ball game.

Jake blurted out, "The less you know... the happier you are."

Not fully understanding where he was going with that blurb, but determined to enjoy the rest of the hour without an argument, I just nodded. He took my silence as a signal for him to keep talking.

"...don't have to be responsible for what you don't know, I guess. It sorta sets your mind free to be happy."

Jake was silent for a moment, then said something else, his way of pushing me for a response.

"So, what you don't know," he said, "can't do you no harm, at least not so as you can see it right away, huh?"

At that instant, I gave up trying to stay quiet.

"Okay... do you even know what you're saying and where do you get these ideas from?"

Jake tapped his right index finger staccato-like against his temple three times, now grinning at me.

"In here," he said. "I watch people and then write down what I see."

I hadn't finished with him yet.
"Uh huh, I think I once heard some female say exactly those same words as you just did, '...what you don't know can't hurt you'."

I wasn't sure if my giving credit to a female for his ideas fazed Jake or not. He looked past me with one side of his lip curled up as if he smelled something he didn't like, then packed what remained of his lunch, and walked back toward the mill. Before going inside the tall white doors, he stopped and spun around towards me. With a wide toothy grin, he gave a departing salute– right hand at an angle making contact with his forehead and heels clicking together once.

"Maybe," he said, "just maybe…I got 'those words' from a 'he' or 'he' got it from me."

"Wait…wait…what?!" I called him back.

"Y—es?"He drawled.

"Did I say I heard a 'he' or "she" say the same as you?" I asked.

"I just figured it was really a he, if you are telling the truth… and you really did hear anybody say anything. With your ways, I never know what the truth is with you, Molly," he said chuckling.

I remembered throwing a couple of pecan shells, hitting him in the back of his head, as he hurried through the doors back to work.

In my mind, I hadn't resigned myself to Jake's partial truth about "my ways"; albeit my lack of response, when he rushed away, was my silent confession to which I would never admit.

****

I wish I could bring someone back after they've died… but then again, maybe not. I'd be too scared to go near them much less talk to them. At the time I brought them back, if I didn't remember that they were dead, maybe it would be okay, then. That doesn't make sense, though. Still, however it would happen, if I could just see them one last time, not knowing for sure when I saw them again that they had died, I'd be happy that I'd gotten one more chance to be with them, afterwards. It would not be until after I'd seen them that I would remember they were gone forever.

I don't know. I wonder if anyone else thinks this way. It would be something to hold on to. Death is just so final. I don't like things to be like that—no matter what—they don't come back. I know what Ma said about the life after, but I just can't get my mind wrapped around any idea that I can't prove by seeing, hearing, or touching. Plus, I don't know of anyone who says they know of someone who was still in existence after they couldn't see them anymore.

I really can't be completely sure I will see my brother again, even if there is that other life; who says the rules are you get to meet back up with your old family again.

I remember when Ma said, "In your dreams…you can visit and never have to go a day without seeing your Ma, even once I'm gone on."

I wasn't so sure that I could or would even want to do that. What's a dream? It's not real. Ma was all for dreams, but it was clear she didn't seem to have or want any other way of meeting up with spirits who had gone on before her.

"It isn't for us to have nothing to do with what's beyond the naked eye. Those things be under the control of the man upstairs," she'd said. "And I'll have no tom foolery with the man downstairs, not in this house."

But I wish there was a way. Give me one last time with my love ones—after they've gone on—to say a real goodbye.

25

Then again, it's enough just trying to make it here in this world from day to day for most folks, so maybe they wouldn't want to come back—not even once.

I don't know.

I walked over to the back room to check on Ma.

I stood in the doorway and looked over at her. My form cast a shadow. She was still awake. My shadow spread halfway across the sunlit room startling her. She swung her head up, her hair flew, and she began rambling again like before.

"I had only a few days before you left to go Boston," she said, "when I had to take the trip to Hardeman County, Tennessee…had to go see about that letter I'd gotten from the stranger. I didn't know him, but I had to go."

Ma talked between rapid breaths. At least she realized I was standing there. I moved in closer.

"They said it may have been your brother, someone who saw him before at the mill, and you know we had not heard from him in a long while–since he left that morning."

Ma said the same words over and over, then she suddenly changed and showed another side of her feelings I never knew existed.

"Molly, did you know I got nothing… never had?" As if searching for something, Ma fingered the frayed edges of the checkered quilt covering her legs.

"People like us–you, me, Jake, and these other share-croppers, we got no power to help ourselves–our children, like *they* can."

I had a hard time looking at Ma. I knew who *they* were. I kept trying to recognize this side of her and the way she was talking about our people and our struggles.

"The law... is their law," she said.

"Yes, Ma." I nodded. I kept my eyes fixed on the headboard above her.

I tried to lighten the mood by picking up a drinking glass from the side table and placing it over my right eye before speaking. "I see you're still going back and forth, Ma, between proper talk and townsfolk babble."

That made her laugh. Was I relieved!

"Put that glass down, Molly!"

Ma swung her legs down and shuffled over to take the glass out of my hand and place it back on the side table.

"Anyway girl, that proper talking, you learned because of me. I taught you to better yourself, keeping yo' heads held high, but still get treated lowly... every moment of every day. Taught you to keep that respectful look on your face and be still, quiet-like. Letting them see what they want to- them thinking people like me and you don't feels the way they do– leastways they don't care– we just better stay out of the way of them getting theirs," she said.

This was Ma? She didn't stop there. She had a lot inside—just pent up waiting for me to come home to say it to.

"I have to stand here and act like it's fine to tear my heart and soul from my body," she said. "'Here you can have my spleen too', cause God made it that way for us —we have to take it. We got to wait on Him to stop

them from cutting on us, but baby, I can't wait no more…
no mo-o-r-re!" she screamed.

Is this the same person who just giggled at me with the glass up to my eye?

What had happened to my Ma?

This was not her. When I'd left home she was love-ly, strong, and confident.

God–her God, never allowed her to think, feel, and talk like this. I didn't know what to do to help her. I couldn't stand it here, near this almost stranger, any-more. I felt my trick leg give way, my feet stumbling, to-ward the front door, looking to get away, if only for a few minutes.

Something stopped me. It held me in place so that I could not reach out and pull the long wooden door open.

"Mama, Ma-a." I'd turned away so she wouldn't see my face. I sobbed so hard that I could barely speak.

I needed someone to tell me—please tell me how to help my Ma.

How long had she been like this?
All I could do was hold her tortured body in my arms. My fingers trembled as I tried to raise her head.

I cried, "M-ma?" And felt her warm frame go limp. I wondered, was she there? Did she even hear me?

Then she whispered, "Why did he leave, Molly?" Without responding to my voice or my touch, she pulled away and stumbled off into the other room again. It sounded now like she was back in Hardeman County, Tennessee talking with the sheriff–and her God.

"Sir, I can't identify that boy, so I telling you Lord, thank you, because I know it's not my Jake." she said.

I got up and followed her, trying to help her back into bed.

"But Ma, what makes you so sure that it was not Jake, especially since you haven't heard from him in a year and a half?" I asked.

I didn't know what made me question her about what she saw. For just that moment, could I have thought she would somehow get back to herself? I don't know, but either way I was wrong. I wish I'd stopped myself.

"I haven't heard from him…haven't heard from him, you say? " Ma, jumped up from the edge of the bed and headed my way. She angrily shook my shoulders.

"Where is he, Molly? Why don't he get word to us? "So tall, lean, and muscular…like his pa at his age. Have you seen him!?" she screamed.

I wanted to get away, but I couldn't. I stayed clear of the front door in the next room, which had been beckoning me. I settled Ma in a chair before wrapping my arms around her again. I tried to hold on tight and wish all of her pain and anger away.

Got to hold on to the moments when you get them…got to wrap your arms around and hold tight….cause you may never get another chance.

I decided that I would not tell her about the 'traveling clothes… ever.

CH 3

(*M*)

I'd gone to bed early the night before and woke up late the next day, dying inside. I decided to take Ma's moods as they come and be ready for anything. After breakfast she seemed better and pointed out an article in a newspaper lying on the table in the kitchen. It was over six months old. That was probably the last time someone brought her a paper. In it was a story of someone attacking the owner of one of the Freedman's stores.

"I think it's the evil—not the people," Ma said. I just let her talk.

"So much has happened to so many people, but not by as many as you would think. There may be three or four White folks out of a hundred who would not treat Negros that way. It don't matter to them that Negro's might get a tiny share of the "big ole pie." I believe those few decide to listen to God."

I only nodded in agreement, thinking that was all she needed.

"So the good folks… well…they try to get around those laws, and bad people who look like them, to do what they know is right. Sometimes when they leave that door open, they get to see all of us…the good in us, too… the way God would have it to be."

I figured I'd better say something.

"Like Mr. Neuman and Aunt Minnie?" I asked.

"I believe so," Ma said.

I wondered if this would be a good time to bring up the secret that I knew. I had suspected a few times that Mr. Neuman was more than just a good man or my self-appointed mentor, but I couldn't be sure.

Mr. Neuman's sister, John's mother, lives just outside of Boston. When she came to one of Aunt Minnie's gatherings, she spoke with me. I was not shocked at what she had to say, but I was a bit surprised, although Jake and I didn't look a lot alike. I had always wondered if Mr. Neuman or someone else had been my real father, but she confirmed it.

Yes, this meant that I couldn't have any more amorous dreams of John Wagner, but that was okay. At least, I was connected to John in some way, even if just another relation, rather than an out-of-town admirer. I think that Dr. Wagner's mother may have already told him about our shared background, before she did me, because after Aunt Minnie's first party, I didn't see him again while I was in Boston.

I'm sure Ma would never tell me everything about her and Mr. Neuman—I didn't expect her to. But at least I wanted her to know that I didn't blame either of them;

they're human, and I'm really not so unhappy about the situation that brought me into existence.

Ma got up and put the dishes in the tub to be washed while I looked outside at buds sprouting on the leafy green pecan tree.

"Let's go outside, Ma."
We walked out into the sunshine. Ma's voice carried into the soft wind, pulling her away from what I wanted to get her to talk about.

"Ah...this world," she sighed.

I didn't know what to expect next.

"Molly, do you remember the books that taught you about history when you were in Mr. Temple's class? The earth and all that is in it is filled with folks who want to take from those who they feel they can."

Before Ma was done talking, I'd gotten distracted by a few sharecroppers' children I'd tutored before leaving home, now older, and waving from across the way.

"Sure Ma, I'm sorry, what did you say?"

"Humph... you didn't hear a word I said, girl."

She repeated herself after giving me a scolding.

"Yeah, Ma, I remember. They call it "Survival of the Fittest." It says the strongest of the plants, animals, and humans survived to procreate the species and races. We also learned something called evolution which talked about man as an animal who evolved to what we see to-day."

I enjoyed acting out a story. I felt sure my eyes widened, as I stooped over, and reached down with bowed arms, stretching my fingers to touch just below my knee; then rising straight and tall with my spine arched and shoulders back to emphasize the "metamorphous" of the species.

I think Ma got the point. "Oh my Lord, girl, you are still somethin' else," she laughed, mimicking my movements.

"I don't know nothing about evolution, or being no animal, though they try to call us that enough," she said, "but man has always tried to beat down one another if he thinks he can take something for himself physically or even get some learning from it to put in his own head."

This past week, it was as if I was listening to Ma for the first time.

"I believe God sometimes has enough of seeing the weak trod on, though," Ma continued, "and puts his ways into some who are open to help others, in spite of what everyone else around them believes."

I thought she might begin to share even more of her thoughts if I kept paying attention.

"Do you think God is a White man, Ma?"

"Now where did that come from?" She looked at me with a raised brow and befuddled glare.

"I always wondered, Ma….just didn't want to say."

"I can't say for sure, Molly. I'm sure most folks think he is, but based on my Bible, I don't believe so. At least Jesus wasn't, not like the White men we see here in Mississippi… that's for sure. But no matter, that picture… the one I still keep hanging on the wall in the front room… it's just a symbol of the man who came as God in the flesh to change the way the world's going. Either you accept him or you don't….but don't base it on a picture– only what you read in here."

33

Ma held up her old leather-bound Bible with the frayed edges. She was a young girl when her mother gave it to her. By now, it was so worn from use that its dark brown cover looked almost tan.

Ma was almost sounded like her old self, so I pushed even more to keep this line of conversation going.

"It just looks to me like God has his favorites. Do you think God cared about the Indians, Ma? I just don't understand what happened to them—why did it have to happen?"

Ma paused for a moment before answering, wringing her hands and pulling a response from somewhere inside of her.

"I don't know either. If you mean some people have more material things than others, well that's true, but it don't last long. I can't say I know why the Indians, who did all they could to fit in, were pushed away from their land. We are some part Choctaw, you know. But you're right. So many died, were deceived or were pushed off. Yet we are still here, in part, mingled though. That's a question I will have to ask when I get through to the other side. Maybe I won't have to ask then, maybe it will be evident, or maybe there was something better for Indian people than this place had to offer. I'll find out when I get home one day."

"I remember something Jake said about it," I said, touching Ma's arm, still trying to keep her engaged and talking. "He said that the Indians weren't as strong physically, but superior in other ways, and White men would always feel threatened by their minds and their ability to adapt to anything, so they "dealt" with them. I am always amazed at how Indians are called "savages" instead of a race of people fighting a war to protect their own land. Jake says they're called "savages" instead of "warriors" in order to make their treatment look more acceptable. He says it will be easier to accept the use of laws, treaties, violence, and deceit to destroy them if they are shown not to be worth saving, in folk's eyes."

There was such a long silence now. I thought I'd made a mistake by bringing up Jake, especially mentioning what he said in the 'present' sense, as if he was right here. I worried Ma might sink back into her strange ways again.

I realized I was wrong when she held up her Bible, placed it to her chest and spoke again.

"Molly, you don't have to agree with me or with everything that's in here."

She lowered her Good Book into her lap, looked up, and then stared at me. It forced me to listen.

"These days, many men and womenfolk are learning to read," Ma said, "so I am sure there are those who write stories that have some beliefs that you do not agree with or understand, but you still enjoy reading their stories—and you do."

I nodded, still quiet, waiting for a signal to speak. But then Ma went even further.

"Things are not always what they seem to you, me, or any other person born of a woman. We only know so much, see the small picture, and never will know it all, at least not to tell of it."

I knew to stop before the conversation got any more convoluting. Ma looked like she finished talking now, and I was grateful.

"I recollect you're right, Ma. I have to get a move on or I'm going to be late."

Feeling it wasn't as cold today, I whipped out a light-weight covering and headed for the door.

"I'll be back soon, bye Ma." I waved.

I couldn't rush off fast enough, still hoping that it was not too obvious that I wanted to get away from such talk about things one could only learn when they're dead and gone.

I would have to try again, another time, maybe get Ma to tell me about her and Mr. Neuman. This other conversation brought her back to me a bit, but not the way I'd planned.

****

The next week, I woke up at daybreak and watched the morning haze fade. Then I walked past the long curtains into Jake's room in the back of the house. Thick dust covered everything he'd left behind, except his cot, hidden beneath an oak poster bed inherited from the Neuman's guest room. They also gave Ma a gold-colored feather mattress, but with Jake gone, she couldn't bring herself to sleep on something new.

I bent down on all fours and reached underneath the raised frame, pulling out a handful of dust. It was so strange. Jake always kept his own area so neat and organized, although he left a trail of destruction behind him everywhere else in the house. I struggled to get up, then wiped my hands and knees off with a rag. Marching over to the kitchen, I grabbed the straw stick broom from the kitchen corner to use the handle to reach under his bed. As I pushed the handle toward the wall, it hit something underneath. When I knelt down to see what it was, I discovered a large, tan burlap bag with a handle facing outward. I reached back and hooked the broom to catch the handle of the bag and pulled it out.

I thought I'd find old clothes inside, instead of what I did.

I unwrapped the brown paper from what was inside and out fell pages and pages of writings on paper Jake must have acquired from his job at the mill. Most of the sheets had hundreds of tiny boxes where numbers belong, but in their place he put words. Some white pages had turned yellow from age or dust, but the top sheets hadn't. They all were numbered, but mixed up. I wasn't sure I would show this discovery to Ma, since I didn't want her any worse off than she already was.

She was lying down on the sofa, and I didn't disturb her. I went to my room with the dusty bag in hand to pull secrets from those pages—anything that would bring me close to Jake.

When I picked up the first sheet from the very bottom of the pile of papers, before I began reading, I resigned myself to the truth—my brother was gone. I'd never see him again, because he thought he had to go away, "to be a man."

CH 4

(J)ake's Writings

The first time I heard the word mulatto a man had come around to the house with a big book, one hot, summer day in July when I was about six or seven years old. He looked at Ma, Pa, and then me and said, "mulatto right?" and set the book down on the table and added the letters on the page with a lot of other words in columns. That was also the first time I'd seen pages set up with rows and columns, like the ones I would later use to do Mr. Neuman's books at the mill. I remember Ma whispering to Pa that the man wrote down our last name and spelled it wrong, but she didn't want to correct him, and I wondered why that was. The man didn't seem to mind me looking over his shoulder at what he was writing down, even though I couldn't make much of anything out. But then the man wrote down something else and Ma said, "His name is Jacob, not Jeremiah, sir." Then the man looked at her like she'd done something wrong and said, "So you kin read, huh?"

But that first word he mouthed when he turned his head to the side and looked at us made me wonder, since I'd never heard it before. I asked Ma what does "mulatto" mean and why did he look at us and say it. But in her way, I don't know if she thought she was protecting me from something, or just didn't have the time to explain, or wasn't even sure herself, she paused after staring at my wide-eyed, curious face and told me to "never mind". After that day, I did just that, but then, I thought the word must have been something really bad that even Ma didn't know what it meant. As I grew older, it didn't take long for me to find out for myself.

I think of myself as a person. If I want to be specific, my mother is Indian and Negro and my Pa was Negro, Indian, and White. But when others look at me, they see something else that registers that I'm a lesser man than they are. What I'm writing in my journals are only meaningless words to them lest someone who looks like them wrote it about me to entertain them with my tales of woe.

*****

I had just gotten enough of Molly's "gumption" to ask that girl at the Freedman's store if I could begin to visit her at her family home. When I first saw her through the window of Grenada County's new Freedman's store that hot summer afternoon, I was on my way to Misterton to pick up the mail for Ma. The sun was smoking through a hazy sky, as it was every summer in the middle of August, with black soot dusting all around with the high winds, and I was hot and thirsty. It was threatening storms later that day, so when I had just gotten off of work at the mill, and before going home, I decided straightaway to head that way to pick up a letter Ma was expecting with news from our kin about a baby being birthed. I looked in the store window, as I passed by, and there she was, standing behind the long white counter that touched her about waist high. She had on one of those crisp, white-collared lady's blouses with a bright, green sash flush around her middle and a puffy little bow in the back. That was all I could see of her, but it was plenty.

I kept walking around the corner, not stopping, so as not to stand there, eyes bucked and mouth open, like some dumb schoolboy. When I got around the corner, I turned around though, and came back and looked her again through the outside corner of the window. I couldn't see her too good from that spot, so picked up my feet and began walking back past the window, knowing that I would have to turn around again if I was to get to Misterton. I stumbled out into the middle of the road before turning back. From where I stood, I could see her brown curls as they spilled out from underneath a matching, blue, silk tignon as she busied herself with wrapping up a piece of cloth in brown wrapping paper. This was my first glimpse of the beautiful girl with the green sash.

I know that I fault Molly for going after what she wants, be it a beau, a better life, saying her peace anytime-anyplace, but I always wished I was like her, at least in some ways. And going after the person I wanted to court was definitely one   of them.   The shameless way she went after Alex, setting up meetings at Milcreek Pond, sending me to hold her place, would have been ridiculous if it were anyone else but her. Yet, she made it seem like the right thing to do.

I was almost eighteen before I got up the courage to go to one of those festivals held every autumn. I had a good time until I got home and Ma and Molly badgered me about how I almost didn't go because I thought it would be a waste of time. That is what I told them. But the truth was it took almost two years for me to learn how to dance well enough to even feel comfortable enough to go. I didn't want them to know that was one of the reasons I didn't go sooner. With all my writings and thoughtful poems, I guess ease on the dance floor was expected.

Anyway, three months before the festival, I was still doing last year's ballroom number and had to fake my way through the newest steps everyone else was doing, because I barely learned the old dance numbers in enough time to go. But it was worth it when I found I could do more than just read books, recite and put some writings down on paper.

The next few weeks, I went out of my way to walk past the Freedman's store every day until I finally got up the nerve to go inside and talk to Sarah. After that day, we met up after she finished work at the store. And after three months, I had gotten her folks' permission to go out together—unchaperoned.

I sat down near Sarah on a seat next to the counter.

"I picked a place where we can be alone for just a while," I said to her.

"Where were you?" she asked.
"Right outside, waiting for you."

"You know what I mean...before now."
"You getting mighty nosey...I had some work to finish up."

"Sorry, you're right."
"Naw, that wasn't right, I don't know why I said that."

"That's okay. You know, I've only started working this last year at the store and we're only a little shop down the way from ole' Mr. Richmond's much larger mercantile."

"Sure, Molly told me. How do you think I found you? I lied. "How do you like it so far?"

"Very much."

After a long silence we'd walked outside— feeling warmed by the balmy breeze. It played with the dark, wispy tendrils that framed Sarah's face. She brought up what I was thinking.

"Jake, do you think they are going to let him stay there? The little shop, I mean."

I wanted the quiet time back again, to keep thinking before I answered, but Sarah was waiting.

"I don't reckon so. I heard Mrs. Neuman say her cousin was going over there for something. You and I know he doesn't go in there just for nothing, and sure isn't going to buy nothing, either."

"I figure it won't last, "Sarah said.

****

I put down Jake's worn writing paper, thinking; I knew he was sweet on Sarah, then picked up another page, since I had the time.

CH 5

Jake's Writings

I know I told everyone, over a week ago, that the only reason I'm heading north this fall morning is to make a better life for Ma, Molly, and me. That was the main reason. But there was more that I didn't tell them. The part that no one knows about but me and her. I know no one would believe my story anyway, and if they did, it is of no consequence. It wouldn't change anything. I'd still be hanging from a tree, beat down, or run out of town at the very least. I first knew there was no going back to the way things used to be after that unusual afternoon at the mill, when he had stepped out to take care of business.

I hadn't thought much of anything at the time when she asked to put my name to her dance card— six months ahead of time. He told me it was fine, but it would've felt more awkward than showing up without a shirt on. I became more relaxed after hearing she was a better dancer than most of the younger girls my age. I told myself to think nothing of it, since he didn't either, that was that. But when I look back on it, I wasn't so surprised by what took place many weeks later, just scared, and I had reason to be. It was approaching the end of summer and not as hot outside. Everything at the house hummed the tune of getting Molly ready for her first Autumn Festival, so I was free from little sister's scrutiny for the most part with my mind relaxed. I was sitting at my desk in a small room out in front of his office when –she came in.

"Good morning, madam. Nice to see you here at the mill today. He is not in the office. He went out, but he will be back in about fifteen minutes. Please sit right here madam...have a seat. I can go out and get you a nice cool drink, if you'd like."

The room was a tiny enclosure– just large enough for only two or three bodies. I got up from behind the papers piled high from the month's receipts to rush out.

"Stop, sit back down, she ordered. I want to talk to you."

"Yes, madam. But I need to make sure you have a nice cool drink first. That's what he would want, I'm sure."

"Now, do what I say. You don't know what he would want for me?"

"No madam, I didn't mean it that way. I'll just sit right back down here."

I froze in the cane back chair for over a minute, sweat lining my palms and forehead, next craning my neck sideways to look outside through the opening to my left, not turning to the right, and surely not straight ahead at her.

I waited.

She needed to tell me what I should do— if I could go.

I could hear her breathing slowly and felt her eyes on me.

She finally blurted out, "just how grateful are you to me and 'him' for giving you this job. You know it was my idea for him to hire you?"

"No madam, I didn't know, thank you so much, I'm very appreciative."

"You must be the only colored boy to ever get a position of bookkeeper in Grenada County or anywhere else in the south, you realize that, of course?"

"I hope I have shown you both that you did fine for the mill by adding me on, madam."

She ignored my attempt to confirm her and his confidence in my work.

"I think I'll have that cool glass of lemonade now," she said.

"Yes, madam," I shot up, almost tipping the seat over. "I'll just go out now for the water and fresh lemons, of course."

"What do you mean, go out? Don't you keep lemons here?"

"Madam, I can get some without any problem. It will only take me about five minutes to get them and get back and have the lemonade ready."

"By that time, he will be back," she said. "No, just get the water and come back with it. How long will that take you?"

"Less than a half a minute, madam. The cool water is right at the pump near the wheel."

"Hurry, I want to talk to you about something important."

"Me, madam? Are you sure?"
She stamped her tiny heel against the floor.

"Oh, just stop it! Go get the water and get back here," she said.

That was the beginning of the end of my life. I wish I could go back and do things differently. I would take a chance at upsetting her by going for the water and returning fifteen minutes later, only when he was by my side, not thirty seconds later, and alone. I thought, if I could just go back. Go all the way back. I would be five years old again, with not just Ma to go to, but also Pa.

*****

I put down Jake's crumpled letter thinking aloud, "What's with all the her's, he's and she's?" Did he think he was writing in code, like he does with numbers?"

I tried reading some more to see if I could figure out if he meant who I think he did.

*****

I turned around to see if Ma was here in the room with me, quoting her daily verse in my ear.

She wasn't here, but she was, in her way.

Then a threatening voice, with a far-fetched notion, reminded me that this was all real—and it was not Ma's.

"Jacob, did you hear me? I said close the door."

"H- Huh?" I stuttered.

I couldn't put that thick, heavy door between us and about 25 men still out there finishing up for the day. The last thing I needed was for them not to see in here, and I know they were watching me, they always are. The thought of it, me in this tiny room with the door closed, and her inside with me.

"Do you want me to call you Jake?" she said, "I prefer Jacob, but Jake will do."

"Whichever you pref-" I began.

"Shut it, now! I don't want to have to repeat myself again," she ordered, before I could finish.

It must have been a while before I completed the three short steps to the heavy wooden barrier. I remember listening to the rubber soles of my too-tight, Oxford loafers squeak with each step.

Ole' Allister Cranston, whose work table sat right outside the door, raised his face up from the crankshift he had purposely hovered over much longer than usual to peer at me. With one eye half open, his mouth parted just enough to reveal tobacco-stained teeth, as the barrier slowly moved forward to seal one side off from the other.

I had barely gotten the door closed before she purred, "You always did have more dark, wavy hair than Enola could handle."

I froze again when she came up behind me, her long slim fingers touching the back of my neck then moving up to the crown of my head. The unrelenting scent of her perfume filled my nostrils.

"The more she cut it the faster it would grow," I mumbled, bringing up Ma, in hopes of bringing her back to reality. My attempt was wasted.

Leisurely, her fingertips massaged the edge of both temples and came to rest behind my ears, moving down again, leaving her warm fingers flush against the back of my neck just above my shirt collar. All the while, she held her other hand firmly atop my left shoulder.

She's got to stop. I told myself.

I'm a man. I can't stand much more. I trembled, knowing what it would cost me to act like one.

She took my quivering as desire and her lips traveled in toward my face.

I tried to hold my legs still from shaking, embarrassed at how it would appear.

A man would meet a woman head on, I thought. I wanted to take her on—at her level— as a man... I knew I could, but the cost...

Still, I'm a man.

A man... I hollered on the inside.

The room closed in around us. It was already small, but now I was suffocating with her scent.

"Hey Jake...back there...hey there boy...we need yo' help out front," Cranston hollered from outside the door... thank God.

Never mind that he was one of several workers who always managed to use the term "boy" to address me whenever the mill owner was out.

At the interruption, she flinched and moved her hand away— which had ventured down my back, gliding atop my moist blue shirt. I had been spared from making a fool of myself —one way or another.

How did I end up like this? I was headed North. All I ever wanted was a good job and a nice house in a city where the sun was warm and shining.

After she strolled out the door, I cleared my mind with memories of the simpler days gone by.

****

After reading that last part, I knew I couldn't show some of these writings to Ma. There were a lot of pages, so I thought maybe another time, I could choose a few of the more 'proper' ones to show to her. That's if I could stomach reading more about some of Jake's surprising happenings myself.

CH 6

*(M)*olly

After being back just a few weeks, I went to bed pleased because Ma was so much better than when I first came home– nothing like Mr. Stratt had described. I think having me here with her made all the difference. I should have been here before now, someone should have sent for me. Then she wouldn't have had to go through this alone.

Those writings revealed so many things I never knew about Jake. I needed a break. I decided to take Ma out to get something to eat early evening the next day. I hadn't even thought about helping with the cooking since I found all those papers under Jake's bed three days ago. The burlap bag was so big and heavy that I'd almost called out for Ma to help me lift it, but I caught myself at the last second.

"Do I look okay?" Ma asked, before we walked out the door to find somewhere to eat.

"Ma, you'd look better than most of those wretches even if they covered your face in mud," I said before thinking.

Then I thought about the description Mr. Stratt gave of Ma covered in dirt.

It wouldn't be easy to get a meal to eat outside of Ma's kitchen, unless we stopped in on one of the neighbors, but I wasn't about to stand for some of their nosey ways, not now.

I'm not sure what I was thinking, possibly that I was back in the North, when I left the house for a prepared meal. We made it to a saloon with an eatery I thought now served Negros—in a separate section, of course.

As I opened the glass, wood-framed door, the little bell at the top rang to announce us. To make things even worse, as soon as we walked in, I caught the discussion drifting up from one of the tables near the kitchen. Sitting there were two powder-faced women I'd remembered from one of Mrs. Neuman's garden parties. It made me not only want to get out of there, but head back on the next train to the ivy-covered brick walls of Boston.

"Well—would you look at her." said one, noticing us, and placing her hand on her hip. "Walking in here like she's a regular person or some lady or something." The other woman at the table scowled, gesturing towards me.

She added, "Somebody must've forgot to tell her she's a niggress."

"Humph, more like a Black/White squaw to me," the first one said.

"Get yourselves on out of here!" Someone else yelled.

I purposely let my heavy purse drop on the polished wooden floor, hoping to drown out the sounds. Then I bent over to pick it up, restraining myself from replacing their words with my own.

"Ma, I know what I said before, but let's go, I'll make something at the house."

When I looked up, there was Mrs. Neuman. She had stepped in front of me, put out her arm and placed her boney hand on my shoulder.

"That's for the best now, don't you both agree?"

She nodded, motioning to the wide-eyed server across the room before adding, "And I'm sure you are all out of any kind of meat that they might eat."

We turned to leave, then Mrs. Neuman reached toward Ma's arm, grinning.

"No greasy fatback or sizzling bacon rind on the supper menu that I can see, Enola," she said.

When I saw her addressing Ma, I stepped in front and moved Ma close behind me, but I was still under control. Nothing she said was going to shake my composure.

Hearing clanging pots and pans in the kitchen, I changed my mind and said to the server, "Before I leave, I only ask that I see the cook, owner... manager or whoever is in charge of this establishment."

"What for?" she asked.

"I'm sure that he remembers me and Ma. Everyone around here knows us... has for years."

"Ho hum," Mrs. Neuman put her hand over her mouth and yawned, while taking her time to speak.

"Are you implying girl that because you believe everyone here knows you they will allow you to complain to the owner about a menu or something?"

Emerging from the kitchen was a tall, white-haired man and a shorter dark-haired, oriental looking one following him. I didn't recognize either of them. They both must have been listening on the other side of the swinging cafe doors, but when Mrs. Neuman raised her hand and waved it through the air like a magical wand, both men stopped, backed up, and returned to their original stations.

Out of her trance, I felt Ma try to push past me to get away, but now I would not let her.

"Did you want something else, Enola, besides the menu?" Mrs. Neuman asked. "I mean, really, if you insist, the kitchen is full of plates to be washed when you're ready."

My hand shot up, but Ma knew what was on my mind, and reached out to clutch it. My fingers just missed the side of Mrs. Neuman's head. Then someone hustled out again from behind the café double doors, just as the two powder-faced women jumped up from their table and came toward us, utensils in hand.

Instead of the white-haired or oriental man emerging from behind the swinging doors, out came a stern pear-shaped matron who acted differently from the rest of the bunch.

Glaring at Mrs. Neuman, who walked off, she said,

"I don't believe in stepping on no one when they is down...Pariah." She said under her breath.

Snickering, I whispered, "Don't you mean piranha?" She said, "You, more than me, know exactly what I'm saying."

I nodded.

"Pariah, Piranha… either works for me," she added.

"How 'bout a Piranha with pyorrhea of the mouth—she be if she keep flapping her gums that way."

"*Wahoo!*" she and I both roared with laughter, which I'm sure reached the other side of the room. Mrs. Neuman came rushing back over with fists balled and eyes pinpointed so tight it surprised me she could see her way.

It didn't surprise me, though, when she hollered at the cook, "Get to work, or you won't have a job."

A few seconds later, Mrs. Neuman stood back and waited her turn, while some younger women in the room struggled to be friendly and cordial, questioning me about my trip to Boston.

Using the other ladies' conversation as a lead-in, Mrs. Neuman jumped back in, looking in my direction without her mouth twisted this time.

"Are you planning to stay now that you're back?"

My neck craned forward at the pleasant tone directed my way. I let go the heavy doorknob I'd reached for, and turned to address my comments to everyone in the room, regardless of whether they truly wanted to listen. Before I could begin talking, however, Mrs. Neuman spoke first as if I was no longer in the room.

"Some say she should have never gone to Boston, and now that she's back, as you all can see, she's worse than before!"

Scrutinizing my mother's employer from head to toe, someone who I'd once thought was my reluctant bene-factress, I gave her and everyone who was listening my opinion.

"I see things haven't changed at all in the time I've been away."

The entire scene was something out of a novel. While in Boston I read a book by an abolitionist named Harriet Beecher Stowe. It was all about Negro's everyday lives as slaves in the 1850s. Harriet Beecher Stowe is White, and the book is one of the most famous published novels in the world. I bet all these people in this room have read the book because Aunt Minnie said it's sold over one million copies.   Now what if Harriet Tubman, same first name, also an abolitionist, had signed her name and photograph to the same story— would anyone buy it?

I laughed so hard at the thought of that group in the restaurant showing up to the Misterton post office, opening the brown papered package, and eyes popping at the other Harriet's dark face, staring at them from the back cover of the book. The tears streamed down my face into my open mouth until I remembered where I was, that I had to focus on protecting Ma, not entertaining myself with amusing parodies involving the people of this town.

I could see I should have said nothing from the start, when others around me, besides the original powder-faced duo, barged into the confrontation.

"Yah!" someone from a back table shouted out, "...'member how she almost burned down the Neuman place at the Autumn Festival few years back... hah, that was you, weren't it?"

"Sho was her. She was coming out that window in her bloomers, I 'member."

Mrs. Neuman retorted, "Now, now…it was determined that my very own cousin started that fire, by accident, of course."

A tall man in blue overalls, who finished his meal, stood, belched, and then hiccupped with a tooth-pick hanging from his mouth, "no matter…*hiccup*… that was her running off, sho' nuff."

I was done laughing and ready to go. If I had a looking-glass before me, I would have seen myself: teary eyed, with a down-turned mouth; a slight young girl standing against the world with only her mother in tow.

Mrs. Neuman stood in front of us, blocking our way, and smirking all the more.

Still, I'd never known her or anyone to lay a hand on me, except that one time at the Autumn Festival. Even then it was a just a touch, almost a caress, in order to make mockery of my appearance.

So when Mrs. Neuman leaned in toward me a second later, I didn't expect to be struck, although I drew back.

Her hand never rose as she leaned over further, craning her neck. She then whispered in my ear something she wanted only me to hear, which set me off.

"You are one fowl, evil, twisted woman, bringing him into this!" I hollered.

Mrs. Neuman stumbled back away from me and grabbed hold of a chair, stumbling. She fell against an empty table as I lunged forward, getting close to her face, raising my hand.

"You can't say such things about him. He's my brother… my brother, that's who he is, and has always been… he would never, never do anything like that! And wherever he may be, it is none of your concern."

Mom came out of her trance again long enough to ask me what had just happened. All the people had moved from their tables towards us, along with the white- haired cook and men from the kitchen area.

I held on to Ma, pulling her out of the eatery with me. I then slammed the door between us and the crowd. On our way out I heard Lena Neuman quip, "It seems Molly doesn't like me."

Someone spoke up, but I'm sure it wasn't in my defense. It sounded like the tall, wiry man in the overalls.

"That's a surprise to you? Anyone around here could have told you that. There are some folks around that there uppity gal likes,…*hiccup* but you sho' ain't one on 'em."

I whisked past the dark horses and lone buggy hitched outside the place to the dusty road, carting Ma along as fast as she could stand to move.

On our way home, I wondered how all that happened with no one stepping in to put their hands on me. There always seemed to be some kind of eerie invisible shield around me when Ma was along. Later, I found out that Mrs. Neuman had become part- owner of the new restaurant, which made it likely she allowed everything to take place just to disgrace us.

The first thing I did after cooking Ma and me something to eat that evening was to get her settled for the night. I then tiptoed into Jake's part of the other room and picked up one of his letters where I'd left off.

CH 7

(J)ake's Writings

When I was a kid, I always knew I was treated differently than the other boys. I didn't write back then, so here, like some of my other writings, is how I recall how things happened.

Out of my stuffy, tight little space, I was present in the middle of a circle of boys at Milcreek Pond in the summer of 1867. Since we were a good distance from Grenada Lake and the Yalobusha River, we all felt this little lake belonged to us. I was, I remember, about age seven, and the only one who didn't have another place to go.

Standing in front of me shouting was the lead boy of one of the makeshift posse.

"You wont him on yo' side?" he said, "...cause I sho' don't."

Another shiny-faced kid had always made a point of announcing to everyone my predicament.

"I had him last time, and he didn't wont to shoot at nuthin' at all."

It didn't bother me none. I'd been left out enough times before….then Rusty came along. Rusty Neuman was just about five years old. Knee high to a grasshopper everyone said he was when he and I first started to come here to swim, leaving Molly, just a baby, and his sister behind howling like coyotes to follow us.

"I'll play along this time, Jake. You can be on my team, and I'll take one of you from yours," Rusty said.

"Nay, Rusty, you don't need to come along and join up cause of me. I can handle things just fine," I told him.

The shiny faced boy didn't think much of anyone taking a liking to me.

"Yeah, Rusty's got his own little ole critter in Jake, don't got no need fo' no four-legged one."

I had heard worse things than what that shiny faced boy– the sun beaming off his forehead– just tossed my way. That's the excuse I gave myself for not going at him with both fists, not aiming for that snaggletooth, turned upper lip face, all the more picturing him in his seat for the lower grade, twice failing Mr. Temple's class.

That was one of many days in my youth that I liked to forget, but this one really was a start of the good times for me. My life began to turn around when I met little Rusty Neuman. I miss him to this day and wonder if he will ever return to the South. I plan to look him up when I make it up North one day and hope that he hasn't changed and will welcome my visit.

One day, I'll show all these writings to Ma and Molly. They might be interested, they might not. I think Ma will; Molly...I'm not so sure. She and I have a strange bond.

****

"Whoa," I laughed hard at that last line, but then thought about how I missed him, and picked up another one of the lined, yellowed pages.

****

Ma had to work two jobs for a short time to make ends meet, so Molly and I learned to do more for ourselves. Still, wouldn't you know it, during her first week of school, Molly got into a scuffle at her first recess bell, before the teacher pulled her and the biggest girl in class apart. I had to leave school early so I could escort her home and keep her out of anymore trouble until Ma arrived.

"Ma, you don't need to wash her head again for another two weeks, can't she just brush all the dirt out?" I asked.

Ma decided that she would let me find out for my-self.

"Go in the back and take another long good look at your sister's head, and remember it rained on your way home."

Molly had defended herself in the schoolyard tussle pretty good, but her hair was now tumbleweed-caked with mud balls and laced with oak tree twigs.

I wasn't sure if I laughed at her, but once out back after a few seconds, Molly started in on me about a girl in my class.

"Saw you looking at that big ole...."

I knew I would never have any privacy again. Everything I said and did would be reported back to Ma every single day. I asked myself...

"Why did she have to start school anyway?"

Molly squinted then rolled her eyes, pulling up one side of her smeared lips to display grayish dirt still crusted in between her teeth.

"I see you looking at her in school tomorrow and I'm telling Ma," she said.

One arm and then the other folded across my chest before I walked up to her, peering at what a horrible sight she made: dirt soaked into every strand of her hair, twigs sticking out, and gray matter stuck between her teeth.

"Go head ugly," I said. "Tell her right now, if you're so all-fired brave."

I knew she wouldn't. I threatened to push her. She screamed.

"M—AA!"

I was close enough that my hand shot up to cover her mouth, then my other hand came up flush against the back of her dirty hair and began pushing her head down into the big wash barrel. Before I knew what was happening, she was waving her arms. My hand came away from her head and she came up choking, spitting and gulping for air.

I felt bad about what I did, and couldn't rightfully understand it, 'cause I didn't have it in me to do something mean to my little sister—no matter how much she irritated me.

Still, I guess it worked 'cause she didn't report back to Ma again for weeks.

******

I'd forgotten about that. I almost drowned in that barrel. I'd tell him that I forgive him for everything if he was still here.

"Well, at least I have these," I whispered aloud, clutching the next few pages to my chest, then placing them on my lap to read more.

******

A few weeks ago we took a family photograph thanks to Mr. Neuman's generosity. I was surprised Ma could take the time away from making Molly's dress for her first Autumn Festival in a little over two months.

Our talk lingers with me now, helping me get through these uncertain days I've been facing lately. "Marriage is more of duty than anything," Ma had said.

I decided to listen to someone older and wiser on the subject, but Molly, as usual, had her two cents to add.

"But I want, above all else, it to be about love," Molly replied.

Before Ma took on that declaration, she moved towards the back of the room with Molly and me to take our positions for the photograph.

"You promise to love, honor, and obey, and God hears you. Then you make the best of it, no matter what comes your way," she said.

Of course Molly had to ask what I was thinking, but I was smart enough to keep my mouth closed while that girl forged ahead.

"But what about love, Ma?"

"Well, love it may come, but I'm sorry, not always. You just do your darnest– utmost best–every day the sun comes up and ask Him to help you do it, cause you sho' can't do it by yourself."

I swung my arms behind my back, looking for a way out of the room and this conversation as Molly tried to pull me into it again.   Thankfully, Ma wasn't finished.

"All this talk 'bout marriage and courting, when most folks get their happiness from things that don't matter much, well it don't require much work—that is on their part. Like filling themselves up on a tasty meal of mustard or turnip greens and cornbread on a fine Sunday afternoon, or drinking a pint of their own squeezed lemonade under a shady tree on their day off, even touching one's face against something icy cool on a scorching hot day. It don't take much to fill yourself up with happiness for a time. It's not so hard to be happy, but it just don't last. Things change, so happy won't hold you long. It feels good while it's happening, though."

Molly and I looked at each other, wondering what road Ma was traveling on with this talk.

"But what about you, Ma, courting and marrying Pa?" Molly inquired.

Ma was not to be deterred, motioning for Molly to "hush up and listen".

"Happiness...hum...," Ma continued, "I figure that may be where the word comes from."

I almost laughed out loud when Molly's eyes crossed 'cause she was staring at Ma so hard.

"What Ma?" she said.

"Happy is being in the moment. Just like when something is happening, it's in the moment too. Happy comes from happening, you see?" Ma said.

Molly still didn't understand.

"I got to ask Jake to explain it later, what you mean Ma, 'cause I'm muddled, especially with you saying it," Molly said.

I laughed then.

It was time to situate ourselves for the photographer, so Ma stopped sharing all about being happy and finished up with her courting marriage talk later that day.

I think I took the courting and marriage advice better than li'l sister, who had been searching for a beau since she was twelve and had finally found one, or so she thought. Later that day, it occurred to me that maybe I didn't need to take time away from the mill for a picture that might show more than I wanted to reveal to anyone...more than most presently knew about me.

There were other pieces of that day I'm writing about, but I don't think I will ever show this next part to Ma. I think I'll take the page out along with a couple of others. There's just some things I can't share yet.

I had put off coming over from the mill just to sit for a photograph, but I finally made it. The portrait taker asked, "Is this it?" when I arrived.

The Neuman's allowed us to take the photo in a room in their rambling white-columned house. The door closed to the parlor behind Ma, Molly, and me, leaving us inside with the photographer. I looked up from straightening my tie and I know I flinched when Mrs. Neuman came into view. Her tongue always pierced like the teeth of a saber-tooth tiger. So I had an idea what to expect. I could see her image in the looking glass on the wall behind the photographer glaring through the mirror looking directly at me. I didn't know how long I looked at her until the photographer called me out.

"Look straight at me, boy, not behind me. There's nothing there," he said.

"Yas, sur," I said, taking on the dialect for no good reason.

I was getting hot in that stiff, white shirt and heavy black jacket and pants, but I wanted to please Ma. She was so proud of how I looked.

"Like a grown man," she'd cried.

The photographer was almost done with us.

"Not sure why I'm here, taking this photo. Must be one of those abolitionist, Indian-loving plantations here," the man snapped.

I immediately looked behind him through the look- ing glass again, then took a quick glance be- hind me, 'cause I was sure Mrs. Neuman was still in the room. She wasn't.

There was nothing there.

****

There were some things about our family and friends that I didn't know about until I talked out- side the family, then asked Ma. For instance, I didn't know our family had a connection to the Choctaw, but my friend Alex even more. Molly still fancies him as a beau, but I'm not so sure he's interested. If Ma mentioned it, I must have forgotten, but I don't see how I could.

It was Molly who told me that Alex realized he was cousin to Ciaok. Alex's grandfather was an authen- tic Choctaw leader. He said he remembers his father telling him years ago about his father knowing Ciaok's pa. Ciaok was there when his own pa got shot for refusing to move West on the trail. Alex said Ciaok's pa might have been willing to go, though he didn't want to leave, not northwest. He said his pa knew that northwest was no way to travel. With all the heavy rains the path would not be passable. Ciaok's uncle and aunts went that way and he learned that they died before they could finish the journey. Ciaok's pa and ma were killed 'cause they wouldn't leave their land to go to a fort the soldiers were forcing them to before pushing them all out west. When Alex painted a picture of what his pa described, I didn't know what to say to him about his cousin, Ciaok. I had known Ciaok since I was knee-high working around Mr. Neuman's place. The fellow was always very friendly, eerily quiet, but obliging. I also knew Alex's pa was a good man around these parts, and a respected one at that. No one told his pa what to do—not for long. He didn't even sharecrop; had his own fifty acres just north of the Neuman estate.

At first, Alex didn't go to school with Molly and me, but he said he didn't fit in with the white folks either. Some called him boy chief—trying to insult him. Anyway, they didn't know him like I did; he was right proud of what they thought was shaming him.

CH 8

(*M*)olly

Out the front door, dark clouds were moving in over the low lying hills.   One whiff of the still,   heavy outside air brought with it smells of livestock from nearby farms a good distance away. Once the water drops passed through the red mulberry and pecan trees out front, hit the ground, and mingled with rich brown dirt, that fresh almost sweet aroma of rain was let go.

It's about 5:00 in the morning and I could hear Ma stir in her bed. I thought I'd better get back to my own bed for a little more sleep. Who knows what I would have to deal with when the sun came up, if I could even see it on this misty morning with the grey sky threatening rain.

I went back to sleep, first thinking about Jake's writings, especially the section about Ciaok.

I later asked Ma where Ciaok was after not seeing him for about a month after I'd gotten back. He may have been a little strange, but now I knew exactly why.

Thunder rolled in from the west, and rain pelted against the rooftop. Ma got up, looking a lot better for the rest she'd gotten after our evening of utter misery at Mrs. Neuman's eatery the evening earlier.

I made her a hearty breakfast of eggs, grits, and buttermilk biscuits with sugarcane molasses. Then I started preparing supper: fried chicken, sweet potatoes, cornbread, and pecan pie. This was a far cry from the fare I'd eaten in Boston, so I knew I had to be putting on weight.

While Ma sat down to eat, I went to the back to check out how much of the food I had room to consume for the day. I took down the looking glass off the wall to have a good look at myself. I'd been home for almost a month and wondered if I'd changed much. I remember what I looked like the last time I stared into this one. Staring back at me was the same oval face framing wide-set almond-shaped eyes, a slightly upturned nose, and a full, wide-set mouth. My wavy, chestnut brown hair was now just below my shoulders. Someone had once given me the nickname 'peaches and cream' and it fit. Alex always said I had a long graceful neck, tiny waist, and long lean legs, and still do. In some ways, I had changed little and had become less modest about my body. So I was standing in front of the looking glass buck naked when Ma walked in.

"Why you looking at yourself?" she said.

"Why not?" I asked.

"Because it's vanity, that's why."

"I don't think so, Ma."

"Then what do you call it."

"I don't know. Maybe it's just sometimes you just want to look at your frame and marvel at its beauty and symmetry, like those painters and poets say, not 'cause you want somebody jumping on it."

'Girl, I just don't know about your ways. What I know is that I don't have time to think about every cotton picking thing people do. Some things are pure vanity.'

"Me neither, Ma. And I don't care about things that make little sense either. If I did, I'd lose my mind for sure. But really, I just want to keep an eye on my shape, that's all."

I reached over to grab my clothes off the bed, looked back through the small window opening, and thought I saw someone coming towards the house. It was time I got dressed anyway, as I didn't exactly think I looked good in front of the looking glass like this all the time. If I stood there long enough and examined every little thing I saw in there, I'd find plenty I didn't like.

"Ma, does Ciaok still work up at the Neuman house?" I asked.

"I believe so, but he comes and goes now. Sometimes he's there for six months, and then he goes on a trip for a month and comes back. Mr. Neuman, I'm told, doesn't seem to mind. He has a man who takes Ciaok's place whenever he's away." "So he's not there? Cause I thought I saw him coming up just now."

"No, I don't think so."

I walked up to the front room and looked out the window opening next to the front door. The sun filtered through the clouds, signaling the end of the rain. The man I thought was Ciaok was stepping over the long dirt path and out towards the trees in the distance.

Across the sky, a golden glow spread as I opened the door and stepped outside, letting the fresh air fill my lungs.

Walking back inside and thinking about the man, I said, "I am not so sure about Ciaok. I know he was one of my most trusted friend's at one time, but he began to act a lot different right before the time of th….the…you know…that Autumn Festival."

I tried my best not to go back to that year that started wonderfully and turned so vile. I still remember strolling home from the schoolhouse on those late afternoons with thoughts of the annual Autumn Festival coming up that late October, my first one. My wayward thoughts had turned to Alex and life took on new meaning when picturing my self-appointed beau next to me in his suit, lean and tall, dark hair combed back, steely grey eyes and that chiseled jaw of his. "How?" Ma asked, interrupting my thoughts.

"O-oh, yes, Ciaok," I stammered.

"Well, it's just that when I saw him last, he just stared past me. He had this blank, faraway look on his face. And right before then Alex told me about a conversation he had with Ciaok and Jake that year that kind of scared me."

I had to make up the part about Alex telling me this story, 'cause I couldn't tell Ma I snuck and read most of what I'm about to say in Jake's letters; not yet.

"It went somethinglike…assimilate or alleviate. Alex said it scared him, the way Ciaok looked when he said it. Everything Alex told me, scared me, too.

"Alex said that he said, "'either you became a part of the White man or you would be no more,'" and that, "'my race will no longer be recognized as one. I won't even be considered human in the world to come.'"

"Alex said, Ciaok then turned to Jake and said, "'You know, Jake, only the strong, the fighters—not the trusting and meek—are going to survive this.'"

Ma interrupted and then stopped my story.

"You know Molly, it's funny you say this because just after the last time you saw Ciaok, he told Mr. Neuman that all these years we had been saying his name wrong. He said his heritage is strong, like the "mighty oak", and that's how his pa named him. Then they came to take a count of people and someone put his name down wrong and told the school that's how it should be spelled. "Ciaok said he is C-i-*oak*, like the mighty oak, and from now on he wants to be called such."

    I thought, I never knew that I was supposed to change what name I called Ciaok by, and neither did anyone else…I don't think. Apparently, Jake didn't know it either. He would've written about it. S o , I went back to finishing—what I told Ma was—Alex's storytelling.

"Alex said he listened out of respect for all Ciaok had been through."

"'Alex,' Ciaok began, "' your ma and pa…they did what I call 'assimilated'–blended in. That's why they survived. Mine trusted, stayed pure, and died. I'm still here, but not for long. And all I have to show for my pride, if I stay and die a Choctaw, is something they call a 'reservation'. Why, I'd rather die than live there that way!

"'I tell you what, we will be fighting in our hearts until we get our land back. It doesn't matter how long it takes. Choctaw will have lifelong wars, not these two-year or six-year wars like the Spanish-American War or the war between the North and South. No, our war is something different. No one recognizes our war. They call them skirmishes and us savages. Why not call it a war like all the others; enemies battling it out 'cause they both desire the same object or want their own way. We have seen the enemy and the White man is he. I know you feel the same. Let's say I name this here war; how 'bout Trusting Landowners vs. Murderous Landgrabbers–the War of all Wars.'"

"Ma... Alex said he and Jake didn't know what to do to help Ciaok and just let him keep on talking."

****

My mouth fell wide open the day I unwrapped the package under Jake's bed. So far, his writings run until almost the day he left home to go North. I knew he was writing all the time when he wasn't doing the numbers for Mr. Neuman—but all this?

I always believed——and still do after reading many of his stories——that my brother does most of his living inside his head.

There's a lot more here that I can't take the time to go through right now. But what I know is my brother would have taken his writings with him if he was able. I have to show these to Ma. Then I can read out in the open. Yes—I need a break, but these writings made me feel closer to my brother. I'd like that for Ma, too.

Still, holding a page, knowing his hand was the last to touch it, brought on a muddle of sweet melancholy I couldn't explain.

I rose from the bed that next day determined to show them to Ma, but it was almost impossible for me to do so, now knowing —almost for sure that my brother was dead.

CH 9

(J)ake

Tennessee-October 29, 1879

Shots rang out in the distance. I knew it was my buddy they were after, but I couldn't think straight. Now I remember; we met on the train. I was determined to leave home for good reasons, all of which only I knew, and found myself lost as to how to speak "southern" once I got to the Grenada Illinois Central depot, on my way out of the god-forsaken town that held all my memories.

It wasn't that I wasn't treated real well at Mr. Neuman's mill, but my whole life, over 20 years, and there I was, with nothing. I know some would say "couldn't have been better...considering."

Only I wanted and needed more than what I could get in this place, especially this part of the South.

****

I didn't know nothing about the mysterious man's past when we just happened to meet at the station after I left Grenada. I was glad to have someone about my age, who looked like me, to talk to in the second class compartment where we were riding.

"So, where you headin'?" he asked me.
"I don't know for sure. I was thinking about Illinois or somewhere like that, maybe Ohio. I hear there's jobs up there, in industry, some chances we don't have down here." I said.

I almost got too comfortable. I was glad no one else was paying us much attention, since I was talking in the voice I learned from Ma. I didn't know if the fella would take offense or not. Maybe think I was trying to be uppity or something. Well, I couldn't change now.

"Sound to me like you ain't sure," he said. "You just running away from somethin', like a lot of us. I gotta get away from here, too. My pa started a store down in North Carolina, but they ran him out. I been all over, since he been gone. On my way to Virginia this time to see what's there. I got me a ma and four sistas still living. I trying to get something, maybe a place, bring 'em with me, 'cause my sisters still young'uns, not ready for no man yet.

Never one for a lot of talk, I just nodded and grunted a few times so he knew I was still listening. He finally stopped. Now he was staring at me, waiting. I had to say something.

"My people are from right here in Grenada, Mississippi. Do you know anything about this town?" I said.

"No can't sez that I do. Just the train stop here is all. I came through once b'fore, but never got off, no need to. Is this anywheres' near Tupelo?" he asked.

"It's a good ways from there, over seventy miles north and east."

"Cause I remember my pa mentioning he had kinfolk in Tupelo, Mississippi," he added.

"I don't know if the train goes that way or not. That's something you may want to know, if you have people there." I said.

We talked back and forth –with him doing much of the talking– for the length of the ride. The people seated in the two second-class cars– which included the smoking car and the observation car with its canopied porch-like open vestibule platform area– walked back and forth past us to the one musty bathroom near where we were seated at the end of the car.

Hurrying pass, was a pretty little girl about eight years old. She slipped and fell over a twisted piece of metal sticking up from the floor, which could have easily injured her. Her food tray flying, she shrieked pathetically, since she surely couldn't afford to get anything else for the rest of the day. Most times one meal a day is all that any of us could afford if we were fortunate enough to travel on a train.

After we sat next to each other talking for over two hours, the stranger reached out his hand.

"By the way, name is Ezra Shank," he said.

We shook.

"I'm Jake… Jake McCray, pleased to know you, Ezra," I said. After introductions, we rode for another 30 minutes in silence.

At that moment, I wondered again if I should continue using that proper talk Ma and Molly instilled in me.

Cause," *it's sho' hard tryin' to go back and forth*", I told myself, taking the luxury of thinking in full dialect.

I wonder if I really need to keep using it here. Although it's now a part of me, it doesn't do me any good while I'm still here in this part of the south—away from home. Best to store it in my mind for future use.

But when I gets to the North I knows I'z gonna throw off this here dialect— never to need it again— cause they's got a different way of treating educated Negros and mulattos , as I heard tell. So's I won't go back and forth so much no more… even in my mind.

Maybe I need to keep the proper talk in my mind while I'm here too, so I won't forget, and for those I'm talking to that I can trust. But they don't want to know my momma and daddy were born free and so was I, that'd make them hate me even more, I suspect. From the looks I keep getting, they don't know what I am, at a glance. If they don't have time to study on me for a while, I don't suspect they'd ask too many questions.

Part-White, part-Choctaw folk, are treated no better than ex-slaves or Freemen, maybe worse, I suspect.

I remember questioning Ma about it a few times when I was about nine or ten years old—just after Pa disappeared. When I got older, I was afraid of the answer.

I always wondered did my Pa leave 'cause he had nothing to give his wife besides someone else's land to live on—or for some other reason?

With me being the man since Pa was gone, all I have to give Ma and Molly is a job at the mill and some flowery words and writing I take to scribbling time and time again.

And the girl at the Freedman's mercantile, I didn't even get up the nerve to court her long enough to kiss her on the mouth. Even though she took to how "fine" she said I looked, it didn't help me.

Molly thinks she's the only one who wants more of something. Difference is everyone sees her more northernlike than me; that maybe she is worth something more than the life we have on the Neuman place. Not me, though. I'm just "right where I should be." I reckon if that's why my Pa left, it may have been partly my fault too. Maybe he wanted a son who would be more than he was, and I gave him nothing to work with. My quiet-type ways, being as I am, he probably wanted to leave 'cause of me. I was nothing to stay for.

At the next stop, Ezra and I both got off the IC train; me first, and my new riding companion a few steps behind. We were getting off the Pullman in Tennessee in what we called Hardeman County, about 40 miles north of Tippah County, Mississippi near Ripley, where the

Tippah County Poorhouse exists for poor Whites. I remembered another one near Grenada County where my friends and I would go by and look at everyone on the porch of the building. They would be sit there watching who passed by or just talking with each other. That was a rundown house for Negros. The nicer one was for Whites.

I wanted to stretch out my long legs and equally taut back. Ezra, who was close to my same height and build, said he'd take a break with me. As we emerged from the back doors of the train in the last car, right before the caboose, I noticed three men with rifles lined up further down along the platform. My new buddy, walking directly behind me, could only see the group when I stepped to the left. When he got a glimpse of the men, right away he ducted back into the compartment.

To check on him, I stopped and stepped back, reboarding the train and brushing past the travelers who were attempting to exit. I wasn't sure what I should do or what was happening. I looked around and didn't see him, so he must have dropped to the brown, dusty floor underneath one empty seat. There were only two extra- long windows on each side of the car, so he had to be way down the long aisle near one of them or watching the armed men from under the seats through thin cracks in the wood frame.

Suddenly Ezra lurched from underneath a grimy, narrow seat, showing stains on his gray trousers and yellow shirt sleeves. He then rolled onto the other side of the train, where he squeezed through a small open window and jumped onto the tracks. The men standing at the end of the platform on the other side, saw him, held up their rifles, and went after him. I kept my mouth shut, like everyone else who'd hurried back into the second class section before the observation car, hoping they would leave us alone to go our way.

The lawmen left one man behind who walked up and told the rest of the Negros to get off the train, letting us step down, one by one, looking each of us in the eye and asking if any of us was with the man who had just run off. When they got to me, I gave the same, "No sir, don't know him at all," response as everyone else.

I could get off then, like everyone else, and was searched..

I told them I was on my way North to get work, before getting back on the train.

I pulled the half sandwich I'd saved from lunch out of my bag and tore off a chunk of bread and meat. I told myself, so I'm leaving this place. I should have left the South altogether when I first turned eighteen. Saying I was making a way for Ma and my sister–like my Pa should've done–was no reason to stay here. Looking out at the lone guard watching all of us, I knew this was not the life I could have had if I was up North. Was I a free man or not? I planned to give myself close to three years, no less, to make a better life and find a nice place for Ma and Molly to come to. I could send them notice what I'm doing once I've gotten settled in a job and a place after about six months. That's the only way I heard it could be done.

Wrapping up the last of the sandwich, I exhaled and looked out the long, smoky window at the burly, bearded guard stationed on the platform with the rifle at his side… thinking, should I try to help an almost-stranger? I've got to survive myself first.

No sooner than I set out to plan my reluctant search for Ezra, the guard from the platform, re-emerged from the shadows, marched right up to the window I had my face pressed up against, and motioned for me to get off the train.

I took my time getting up. Weighing each step, which got me to thinking about Ezra and how I wished I wasn't such a friendly sort. Could he be a wanted man? I wondered. Running zigzag cross the South from Texas to the Carolina's, funneling through Mississippi now mak- ing his way through Tennessee? Probably not.

Fear. That one word explained why I find myself at this junction, debating whether to help a fellow like my-self. It could be me. I pulled along the suitcase with all my belongings I'd lugged on the train, 'cause I'd re-fused to leave them behind.

That hazy afternoon, as I stepped off the Illinois Cen-tral train platform in a Tennessee station, hear gunsh-ots fading as the sheriff's men fanned out further away from the busy depot. They were heading southeast.

****

The bullet must have barely grazed my leg, 'cause I wasn't bleeding. I wasn't sure who shot me. Maybe one man had backtracked or there were more than three hunters. And one knew me. How?

By the time I caught up with Ezra, he said they'd shot at him while he was hiding in some thick brush. He thought one said my name. Was he hallucinating? The wooded area was so dense–with uneven terrain, and towering oak and pine trees–that the bounty hunters trampled through twice before spotting him.

Hard to believe that Ezra took a moment to say goodbye and wish me well before he left the train back at the depot. "May the Lord keep you," were his parting words. They reminded me of home and something that Ma would tell Molly and me.

Now that I'd caught up with him again, all talk was just madman ramblings–from a ways off– of how we could save ourselves from being shot dead.

I wished he'd told me he had people on his trail. Had he given those bounty hunters reason– besides being a Negro–to come after him? I knew though; it wasn't nothing he had to do that was so bad. Maybe got a job those folks felt was rightfully theirs, that's all.

""Ugh!"...was the only thing I could muster when he– and then I– fell into some kind of smelly black, yellow and red muck about a mile up into the woods. With bounty hunters possibly still in pursuit, getting good and filthy was the least of our worries.

I must have run for hours and it looked to me like I was heading back to my home where I came from. I couldn't be sure if Ezra was still behind me or not. If so, I knew we were somewhere back in Mississippi by now.

"Ow...oh hell!" The pain brought me back to reality. I had thought it was barely a surface wound. Now, I'm really starting to bleed. Got to stay up. Got to keep going...make it to one of those rocks between the trees on the side of that stream.

I'm going to bury some writings under this large rock on the side of the mountain, here midway up, and if they ever find these papers, Ma and Molly will know that I loved them and they could be proud of me–no matter what happens.

"Oh God, the pain!" The bullet may have done more than graze my leg. Why so much blood? I can't stand this no more. Are they coming now? Got to stay quiet… so I can hear them. Got to find some strength to drag these, oh my God, look at this bloody leg, got to get over to the other side of those trees ahead. Don't want them to find me here, out in the open, near the rocks, can't let them find me.

"Ma-a-a." I heard a guttural sound escape from my insides.

"Oww!" I ripped the bottom half of my shirt and tied a tourniquet around my upper thigh, to help the pain subside and lessen the blood flow.

"Humph…little sister… I got more gumption than you think."

What made me say that at a time like this? I heard no one behind me for at least ten minutes. Maybe they'd given up the chase, since it was almost too dark and they won't be able to see anything.

"Hoot…Hoot."

The sun should be setting now. The familiar sound of the spotted owl rustling in the tree above, made me wonder if I was ever gone see Ma or Molly again. I could hear my l'l sister correcting my speech. Not Ma, though. She wouldn't be saying nothing, just touching her hand to my forehead. I sat quiet a long time hearing nothing else.

Twigs suddenly began crackling and crunching on the cold ground far behind me. Then, I heard three voices; sadly one was very familiar… it was Ezra, my companion from the train.

"I tells ya don't know what yo' talkin, 'bout or what you wont," I heard him say."

"I ain't the man you wonts, I tells you!" He pleaded.

"I'm gonna tell you for the last time, hand it over!" The unknown voice said.
"I can't see him clear…can you?" Another one said.
"Well enough."
Then shots rang out.
Crack…Crack… Crack.
The sun was long gone.

CH 10

(J)

When I woke up, the first thing I saw was half-dried blood caked on my trousers. I didn't know how long I was out, but it was now daybreak. I remember bounty hunters shooting at me and a man I met on the train. I recalled the last shots I heard. Had they missed and mistaken me for dead?

Someone had emptied my pockets. Clothing in my backpack and everything I'd thought valuable, all strewn everywhere. I struggled to pull down an extra pair of trousers that were hanging from a tree limb.

Scrambling up, I managed to get my bottom clothing off and wash what were two flesh wounds on my leg, along with my trousers in the nearby stream. It was still warm enough out to have my outer clothing off for a while, before wrapping my leg with a ripped undershirt.

Figuring the men to be long gone by now, I put my shirt back on and some other trousers over the wrapping, and then headed off. I wondered if I should try to find a way to change some aspects of my physical appearance. After going through my wallet, it looked to me like I needed to scrape together money–cause they took that. On my way back, I saw no sign of Ezra—whom I suspect was dead—but it was now every man for himself.

With no money, I couldn't get back on that train heading north. I couldn't stay in Mississippi if I was still being hunted. I didn't want to go back to the town at the last stop either. My only option was to try to get on the back of an idled freight car and head to the next busy stop north, where I would be lost in a busier town where no one would recognize me.

The freight pulled into the next stop after Hardeman. I could see between the slats that the depot was small. I waited for two more stops until it reached the town of Memphis. Even though they'd lost three-quarters of the residents in the Yellow Fever epidemic of '78, this town was still big enough for me to get lost in. After limping off, I ambled for about 30 minutes, and made my way right outside the door of the first busy establishment. Clearing my throat, I wanted to get the attention of the proprietor, who was standing right inside the doorway, before I stuttered.

"H-how's ya s-suh?"
He was a stout, dark-haired, mustached man, I judged to be about 40.

" Hum, what? Yah?" he said.

" I seez...yes'm sir, I's good with numbers."

"What in hell do you wont? You a Negro? Move on." He said, turning and flicking his thumb.

I thought how shamed Molly would be if she heard me talking now, but I needed to get my hands on some money –anyway I could.

"I used to hep one of the biggest mill owners in the south with his books. Yas….I was his right hand boy. Don't know how's I gits so good with numba's and all, my ma sez I was surely bon' that a'way. You give me a piece a paper with any kinda numba's on it and I kin figure 'em out. Jes lik dat," I said.

"Well, what else can you do?" he asked.

"Why if yo interested in someone who can writ a bit of words for someone to play on that there piani over there, I kins do that too."

"What about cleaning up?"

I nodded up and down, letting go a hardy laugh, slapping my knee for effect.

" I'z 'spect I kin do that too, if yo' wantin me to. But after I works with them numba's and those piani key wuds, yo may changes yor mine, yez, for 'shore you will, I do 'spect," I said.

"Humph, we'll just see about that. Let's get in the back. "

I grinned, held my head down and kept my eyes half shut, as I nodded my respects to the gawking public on my way to the back with him.

Ha… Ma would pitch a fit if she knew I was just hired to figure the books for a saloon and gambling spot.

I better wipe this smirk off my face before anyone starts to thinking too much. I hope I didn't overdo the dialect.

"Here," he said, shoving me a large box off the shelf. "Deliver this here package to the postal office at the station."

****

It was a new year. Two months and three days since I left Ma and Molly in Grenada, and I still hadn't sent a single post to either of them, though I'd traveled to the post office almost every day. Was it completely safe just yet? I wondered. Some sheriff might give Ma and Molly a hard time if I contacted them, and I didn't want either of them to have to lie for me.

The man in the booth looked up as I approached the arched brick opening.

"You got yourself a package, boy?"

"Yas, suh. This be another package from the saloon, suh. Mr. Finch asked that it be going furst class."

Having given up shaving for a while, I was glad of the natural dark covering casting a shadow along the lower half of my face. Never one to like hair anywhere but on my head, it didn't take long for it to grow, with me no longer attacking stubborn hair follicles every day with pa's old razor and shaving cup he'd left behind. Anyone who saw me even a month ago might not know me now. The mustache and scruffy looking beard had me looking more like 35 than 20. My palm slid against it now, feeling rough, dry and scratchy. This was the price I would have to pay to make enough money to get up North, then I will be out of hiding permanently.

The sun should go down in about an hour. I had to rush to get back now to get today's take figured out. Finch wanted all the money out of sight, recorded and locked up before darkness set in. He couldn't trust anyone in or out of town not to rob him once we're under the cloak of darkness.

I didn't look up rushing to get back.

"Dang," I said, bumping into a little white girl standing on the walkway with her mother. *God, help me now. Tell me what to do.*

"Sorry mam, I begs your pardon, please step ahead of me, may's I carry you bags for yo," I said.

"No just move on and git outta of our way," the girl's mother ordered me.

I felt like this was even a worst time than I'd spent living in that little town in Mississippi. This was the real world, the way things really were.

I bowed in a deep respectful bend, keeping my eyes away and head down.

"Yez'm for shore, madam, I'z so sorry. I is." I said.

" Yez, I wonts ta thank ya," I said again.

As I walked away, I could almost see my sister Molly twisting up her face at me.

Now that I had the job for a while, I set to doing all that I could to make myself indispensable. I ran errands at breakneck speed, then swept and mopped the floor of every speck of dirt and dust my eyes could perceive.

Somehow, I'd gotten the owner to rent me a tiny back room upstairs in the furthest corner of the saloon where I worked most days. I think it helped most folks couldn't tell who my people were with just one glance. One afternoon, while the salon was closed, I snuck downstairs and sat down at the piano. I'd taught myself to play years ago on the baby grand in the Neuman parlor. Well enough, so I was asked to play at school and on Sunday mornings in Ma's church.

As I fingered the keyboard, the owner walked in and I jumped up, knocking the seat back to the wall.

"Sit back down, and keep playing," he said.

From that one day, there was an addition to the entertainment in that place and a few others in town.

I didn't think it would earn me the money I needed, but when I learned that all owners will pay me more if I added piano playing to my list of duties, I ended up playing the piano regularly.

As entertainment, my regular saloon and the other five in town offered dancing girls, some of whom occasionally or routinely doubled as daughters-of-sin. The saloon where I played piano about five days a week, offered Faro, poker, brag, three-card monte, and dice games. Two of the saloons were located less than a mile apart, in either direction. They had even more games like billiards, darts, and even bowling that brought in more money for the owners. Not every saloon hired a regular piano player like me, but they'd compensate by having more play skits.

There was one Irish bar up the road where there was no piano player, but where a play skit was happening this week and even proper women could get service through the front door.

Like the first place that hired me, they all had the pair of "batwing" doors at the entrance, which was the easiest way to recognize it was a saloon if you didn't know. The doors had those double action hinges allowing them to swing in and out and extended from chest to knee level.

One of the saloons where I worked occasionally was elaborately decorated. It featured fancy glassware, and oil paintings hung from the wall. Their hard liquor was better than this one, some of the whiskey was even imported from across the ocean. I heard the folks coming into that bar ordering high class, mixed drinks like Claret Sangaree or a Champagne Flip, not whiskey or beer all the time like most places.

CH 11

(J)

It was on a Thursday afternoon, a week later, that the man named Henry came into the place for the first time. I learned he was out of Virginia, but was in town for business. He stood out from the others since, most of the high faultin' folks went out with the Yellow Fever. There were more poor Whites than anything these days, some Mexicans, and Negro's, but the poor Whites were now running most things. Henry came into the saloon up to four times in one week, before he ventured over to the piano where I was playing, and introduced himself. I thought it was unusual, since none of the White men who patronized this bar or any of the saloons, thought it necessary to make themselves known to the "Negro" in the back playing the piano.

After talking to him in my practiced dialect, he somehow figured out it wasn't really comfortable for me and not my usual speech.

"What's your name," he'd asked.

"It's Jeremiah, suh." I told him.

Our becoming acquainted with one another began from there. Although more ruddy looking than some, he was still blue-eyed, with dark yellowish hair, so there was no mistaking his background or getting too comfortable with him.

Once I'd forgotten and left something out on top of the piano. It was a writing pad that I kept on me at all times.

No one usually came back over into the corner where I played. If any of the patrons had a request, they would just yell out from their seats. But Henry was over there that day, as he had been a few other days that week.

When I walked back over to the piano, Henry was looking through the pages of my pad. He was as tall as I was, but with a sturdier build, and had to bend over some to see the writing clearly. By now, we had become pretty friendly with one another, so I wasn't worried.

He wanted to know why I didn't write more about all the things that happen to my people... the violence against them and the lynching.

"Why would you ask me to write about that?" I asked.

He looked like he didn't understand my reaction to his interest in that subject.

"Just a question, I know that you like to write, I've seen evidence of it in your room. You have pages and pages of the stuff."

I put down the paper I was reading, picked it up and put it back down again. I'd forgotten, I let him come to my room the other day, when he asked. What else could I do?

"I could never write about killing, death and violence for folk's reading enjoyment. Papers like *The Colored Citizen* already inform folks about those goings-on. There is already enough talk and writings of that in the world for me. A lynching happened just down the road from me back home, a week before I left," I told him.

I almost said, *Another man who was with me on the train, hunted down and shot dead, I believe.*

I stopped first, not wanting to share too much about myself. He looked away and then down at his fingers locked together. The light from outside reflected off of his copper-colored hair, combed straight back then to the side, reminding me for a moment of a younger Mr. Neuman. I kept talking, careful not to reveal anything, as I filled the silence.

"No, I don't need to write about these things over and over again…it just is. No need to draw more tears from reading about it. Rivers of tears are already flowing from the real goings-on. Writing about living this everyday life is sad enough to read about most times." I said, thinking about the bag of papers I'd left at home under my cot.

My reasoning seemed to satisfy Henry, so we changed the subject and went to talking about the troublesome relatives he was visiting in town. It felt good to be able to laugh and talk about some else's life, for a change.

CH 12

(J)

In early March, I got a chance to follow Henry to one of his family gatherings in town, serving as a waiter. Since they needed a few extra hands to serve drinks and wait their traditional over-sized family table, I told him I'd help out when he'd offered good pay.

Residing in a home of the few, still well-to do, I had the pleasure of seeing and hearing Henry's Uncle Matthew and family whom I'd laughed about a couple of months earlier.

"I read in the paper yesterday that two Negros were stripped of their stores because they couldn't keep up the property as they should. The town took their stores and made them work there as stock boys. One tried to get a lawyer to represent him. They found him dead the next day. His head was bashed in and he was lying behind the mercantile," Henry's uncle said, looking around the dining table waiting to be served.

One of Henry's aunts, whom I learned was this event's hostess, lived here alone. She offered her own opinion of the newspaper story her brother brought up at her dinner table.

"I wonder what happened. That's what comes of letting them hold positions on the city council. It's best that they work the land, instead of trying to own or run it. There are always such dreadful problems for everyone when they do."

Again Henry's Uncle Matt took his turn, and offered his longtime opinion on the subject, as if it hadn't already been clearly expressed.

"Those animals. That's all they are good for," the uncle said, looking directly at me.

With one hand, I laid his plate of lamb and kidneys down in front of him, while holding his drink to set in front of his knife.

"What is that supposed to mean?" Henry said.
His wife, sitting nearby, pleaded with him. "Please don't Matthew, let it be this time."

He didn't.

I stepped back away from the table still holding his glass in my hand, thinking this is the family I thought was funny?

"Why do they think they can come from nothing, those beasts," he said, "and take what we worked so hard to get and build?"

Henry pushed his plate away from him to the center of the table. "According to Darwin—if you will—we are a just as close to the 'beasts of the field'."

Henry didn't stop there, standing up, then sitting back down again.

"Why do you think you still love your meat cooked rare, always?" He said. "Take a good look at the blood still present in that piece of lamb sitting on that elaborately designed place setting in front of you."

Henry pointed with his own knife in hand, "like a lion ready to chew on its conquered prey."

I appealed for calm in my mind, hoping he would somehow hear me.

Please don't speak up for my benefit, I don't want to be in the middle of this.

Henry's fiery-faced uncle threw down his fork he had aimed at the succulent leg of lamb sitting on the gold- rimmed plate. The platter was pressed against his enormous stomach as it rested on the edge of the table.

"You're insane. Where is this coming from? Y-you talk like you prefer them to us," he said.

Henry put aside his glass and looked directly at his uncle, and then at all the other relatives at the table.

"It's not a matter of preference. It's a matter of ignorant talk deserves an equally ignorant response.

"You're the ignoramus," Henry's uncle shouted, "Better ignorant, even insane, than a traitor to your own people!"

Henry sighed loudly, his eyes rolling back.

"Why waste your Darwinist ramblings on one who has no taste for it?" He said.

"What?"

"Nothing."

Henry sighed again, got up, walked over to his uncle– who was still sitting– and then spoke vehemently.

"Listen uncle, I love my people, don't you ever forget that! We were made above the animals, but so was every other human being. You know where I stand on this!"

His uncle looked up at him. "Say what you want, I know animals when I see them, and *they* are still beasts."

Henry became silent, then leaned over and whispered something into his Uncle Matthew's ear.

Whatever Henry said, made his uncle lurch up. The older man shoved his opinionated nephew back against the wall, then threw his full dinner plate across the room. The crystal chandelier above the dinner table shook.

"Hell, we're leaving!" He roared.

Henry reached his arm out and placed his hand on his uncle's shoulder.

"You don't have to leave, uncle."

The man shook violently trying to jar Henry's hand loose, causing his neatly combed gray hair to fly.

"I do. And so will the rest of my family."

As he exited the dining room, Henry's Uncle Matthew stopped to deliver a final verbal punch.

"If you aren't one now, you would have made a good abolitionist 20 years ago."

A less apologetic Henry responded, "Thanks, Unc'. I'll take that as a compliment."

The duel between uncle and nephew continued to the front door.

"I know that you are a fool and I hate what you are saying, but you are still my sister's son, so I'm warning you. Stop telling those blasphemes of yours around here. I can promise you, talk like that will get you maimed, and even killed."

I gulped down the drink still glued to my hand and did my best to stay out of sight, while saying one of Ma's prayers for my new friend, Henry.

After the evening's drama, I thought I'd write to Ma and Molly when I got back to my room at the saloon. There would be no mention of the melee I'd just witnessed.

CH 13

(J)

So much time had passed. I guess I'd gotten comfortable, I can't say. All I know it's been a little less than a year and a half since I first came here and found work. So I wasn't surprised as I was just getting off work, when Mr. Oliver the new proprietor came by and asked me to fill in day after tomorrow, my usual day off.

"You can take off tomorrow, instead." he said.

Early the same evening, a reddish-brown man wearing a blue shirt and dark trousers appeared through the swing doors and called out to me. I recognized him immediately.

"Jake…J-Jaco…?"

"Cioak?? Yeah it's me…it's me….Jeremiah…Jeremiah!"

I stopped him before he could say my real name again, pulling him aside where no one could hear us.

"Just call me Jeremiah, nothing else, please," I whispered.

Cioak had been Mr. Neuman's friend and sort of companion-servant. When I left home he had returned to Grenada after being away for years. It made me nervous running into him here. Since the last few months before I left home, I'd heard that he had been acting strangely, standing close and yet not hearing a word. He was even forgetting his duties at the Neuman's and had even changed his name from 'Ciaok' to 'Cioak.'

"Oh God," Cioak said, "Your ma has been looking for you so long. Oh, and by the way, I'm going by the name of Ciaok again."

Good, I thought. His own name flip-flop should keep him from questioning why I was using a different name.

We shook hands, then he grabbed my arm and we hugged each other for a good while before I pulled away.

"I was riding through town and just happened to stop in this here…what'd you call it?…SteerHouse saloon for a drink," Ciaok said. "It's coming up on two years…my friend. Have you been here all this time?"

I drew back even more and went to slap him on the back– shocked, noticing tears in his eyes. We talked freely for a while. I avoided explaining myself.

"W–ell, would ya look at these two?"

A few regulars, I'd seen in here many times, were sitting off on the side of the bar when Ciaok first came in. They were exchanging nods. But I wasn't familiar with two men making their way across the room, past tables and chairs, over to the far corner toward Ciaok and me.

"What is this, the Indian-slave reunion?" One winked, turning to his friend.

At that, laughter erupted from the few patrons in the room. I was glad that it wasn't the late evening crowd. Things could have been worse.

Luckily for Ciaok and me the saloon had just reopened for the night and no one else was there, but the bartender, the few regulars and these two strangers. I hoped Ciaok would keep his mouth shut. My hope died instantly.

"Well, we sure ain't Buffalo Bill, now is we buddy?" Ciaok said, turning towards me for confirmation.

I froze. *Why'd he wanna keep this going?*

Ready for a battle, the men turned their sights on Ciaok. "Hey injun, what would yo Indian chief grandpappy and squaw say about you taking up with this here nig–?"

I didn't want to get into a skirmish, especially when I was trying to keep my cover. Why would I bring attention to myself? All I had wanted was to make enough money to start over again in the North.

I stood still, stoned faced, not saying a word. I hoped Ciaok would do the same—so as not to reveal my real identity.

"Look boys…" Ciaok said, pushing his freshly cut hair back, "why don't you just pull in your horns and hitail- it outta here?"

Ignoring him, one–a bearded, grimy cowpoke slurped down his drink and made his way closer towards us, almost tripping over the stool in front of him.

"Is ya blood brothers?" He asked, letting loose an enormous belch.

Not to be outdone, the other one broke in.

"I declare, can't narily tell a one from da other," he said, pointing at me. "Looks to me as close to injun' as that there one with dat dark hair and yellow-red skin of his."

That personal observation must have tickled the ornery pair to the core, 'cause they were laughing so hard one kicked the stool over, while the other one smacked him on the back grinning and spitting on the floor, marking his territory.

I moved, walking a few steps around them, but both men, determined to say their piece, jumped over and blocked my path.

I glanced back and Ciaok was coming up behind me.

In that moment, we connected eye to eye, searching for some kind of plan—fast.

I spoke first.

"Howdy ho… ya reckon he and me jis' might be kin at dat!" I said to the scraggily pair.

The men stopped laughing, grinning, and spitting long enough to listen to my overly-contrived thick southern dialect.

"If ya'll recall I heard tell his grandpappy was given a treaty by ole President Jackson, but he turned around and said it was God's will for the destiny of yo' people and dis here injun's folks to go they's separate wez. Well, my folks had come long 'round dat dare time his kin was bein' pushed out."

Tobacco juice oozed from the corner of one's mouth, while the two imbeciles looked at me with their mouths hanging open, begging me to add a little more to this tale that this tale that I didn't even understand.

"So his people be mostly gone now, but we just mayhap meet up for a spell," I added.

The bearded one egged me on.

"Yah?"

"Now this here injun, he's still here fo' a spell, while yo' people got their destiny– and all this land awayz from them. So there's no need to fight, wez all happy now," I concluded, with a gigantic grin and then elbowed Ciaok in the ribs, to do the same.

The two wary cowpokes stood there scratching their heads, staring at one another, with a blank countenance on their faces. I hoped this meant that I'd confused them, and they would stop harassing us and just move on. But Ciaok wasn't ready to stand down, just yet.

First looking at me, he then turned towards them, and said his piece.

"What I don't understand from yo' story is why God and he," Ciaok said, pointing his finger at the scraggly one with the beard knotted below his chin, "always got the same ideas as to what should happen to my people and yours."

He then turned back toward me, as if they were not even there.

"Ever wonder that?" Ciaok continued.

I thanked God Ciaok didn't slip and say my real name, but knew I had to stop him before he did. He stayed facing me, ignoring my hand raised for him to stop saying any more.

"Why don't God have the same ideas as you and me sometimes, huh…huh?"

I shifted my weight from the left foot to the right, watching the bearded man's mouth begin to twitch as Ciaok shifted to him now.

"I mean, I believe in your God," he continued, as the other cowpoke turned red, "but I don't think He is wanting to be told what He thinks and wants all the time. 'Cause that's what you do, you reckon? You say whatever you think or want for yourself and everyone else is what God thinks and wants too, or that's just what you want us to believe you believe."

I didn't want to disrespect my friend from back home, who was more than twice my age, but I had to do or say something to get him to stop.

"He don't mean nuthin', sirs. Hez a lil' strange in da head," I said, throwing my finger up to my temple fast as I could.

Ciaok chuckled. He must've finally paid notice to my "Southern dialect" and found my actions humorous as my index finger rushed to my head so hard and swift I just missed poking my eye out.

"You may be a bit Choctaw, but you sure don't sound or act like it," he joked.

I forgot where we were and hee-hawed right along with him.

"I reckon there be a sprawling valley twixt being some Indian and all Indian." I said, howling, still pointing at my head.

But before I could get my hand back down to my side, the scraggly partner yelled, "dat gum it," and picked up a tall, wooden, round back chair with an upholstered seat and slung it at Ciaok's head. He ducked and the chair crashed into the back wall, breaking and splintering into pieces.

I leaped up onto and over a table, just stopping Ciaok before he came up behind both men with a whiskey bottle in each hand aiming for the back of their heads.

The bartender was cowering behind the counter until a flashy dressed woman in tight lace-silk dress and a feathered hat sashayed through the front door.

I grabbed Ciaok by the collar and ran out past her, as far away as I could get from there. I let go of him when we got out of the door, but stayed close behind, shoving him forward until we had traveled at least 500 paces down the road. Before I could head home, I noticed someone peering out from behind a long clapboard. I knew who it was as he stepped forward, and thought it would be best to acknowledge his presence, to not arouse any suspicion.

Ciaok and I slowed our pace as Henry trekked out onto the road coming from the inside of one of the other crowded saloons.

I spoke to him in the usual Southern dialect, although he'd earlier deemed it as counterfeit.

"Mornin', Mr. Henry, suh."

Wiping his mouth with the back of his hand, he looked as shadowy as the long, gray strip he'd stepped out from behind. He walked past Ciaok and me without saying a word.

Ciaok turned to me and snickered when the man got just ahead of us.

"You're invisible," he sneered, "'less he's looking for someone to take the blame for something."

I wished Ciaok would keep quiet. As if he didn't know the protocol—I had to play along. The man doesn't know me, at least not today. There may be others he knows somewhere around here watching and it would make him seem lowly to other gentlemen in his position. I only said "suh" thinking that it sounded respectful enough for the others and Henry would still know that I saw him.

I play along, well.

I had hoped this new encounter wouldn't get Ciaok going again, but my mind braced itself when he ran ahead and followed Henry into the boardinghouse at the end of the street. I had to go after him. I couldn't take the chance he would blow my cover and get those bounty men back on my trail.

Ciaok got going as soon as we made it inside, looking around the room for "Mr. Henry," I thought. He looked at me, said nothing, and continued stepping through the establishment as if I didn't exist.

We sat down in the back, and Ciaok turned to me, picking up where he left off.

"Could it be just your fear of men like him and those in this room getting wind of the fact the you want to be something other than a piano player or a porter and them doing everything they can to shove their boot up your ass by making sure you face every obstacle they can create? Why? You'd think they have enough, wouldn't you? They never get enough, and as far as you're concerned, it's part of their destiny to make sure they keep an eye on you with your thinking. You got a right to aim for something other than what they're offering."

"Ciaok, they're not all that way," I countered.

111

I wanted to say something more, be a part of this almost one-way conversation, but all I could see was Ma looking at me with her finger pointed saying, "We don't think his way. That's why he can't understand what you just said. He didn't even listen to you. You know why? 'Cause God done so much good for us. So we find some good in everyone, 'cause there is good in everyone. Some bad, yes, but good too, cause we made in His image. Remember what I taught you. Men like Mr. Elijah Lovejoy all the way to our martyr president, Mr. Abraham Lincoln. There are many men like them, including Mr. Walter Neuman. That's why, Lord willing, we just may go north one day if that's what it takes to get your thinking right. More people like those kind of people there."

In my mind, I answered, '*I hope to be on my way there soon, Ma.*'

It was after midnight. I grabbed Ciaok's arm and traveled out the door around back and up the outside stairs to my room. He pointed out his beautiful palomino hitched to the post in back. I remembered it well. He said he was worn out from the ride and Memphis was to be just a quick stop, but since running into me he might stay a few days. I didn't ask him where he was going or coming from, since I didn't want him asking a lot of questions about my predicament.

When we got upstairs to my room, Ciaok sat down and pulled off his boots. Immediately, a foul musty odor filled the room. He then stepped over and pulled two handfuls of ashes from the dead embers in the wood stove dropping them down one boot and then the other.

"What'd you do that for?" I asked.

"It's for my condition," he said, now pulling off his woolen socks.

On his left foot, three short toes were topped with yellowish, brown nails. On the other foot, the toenail on his big toe was brown and crusty looking.

"If I drop these ashes in my boot," he said, "and rub some on my toes, along with a little menthol, it should be right in about a year or so."

He put his dusty shoes to the side and lay down between two chairs pulled together. I wished he'd kept his boots on; the room smelled a lot better when he did.

CH 14

(J)

As I had the day off, the next morning we went out to get breakfast and saw Henry Lawson again, but this time he walked over to me. Either way, I played along.

"Good morning, Jeremiah. You did a great job helping over at my aunt's house last week. I just wanted to let you know. May I sit with you and your friend?"

There was a man standing near the bar being scrutinized by everyone. I didn't know who he was. Henry didn't recognize the stranger, either, but that didn't stop him from making his way over to us from way across the room. Before we knew it, the man had pulled up a chair between Ciaok and Henry, and joined in our conversation.

"Listen," the stranger blurted out, "let me tell you something about the Confederacy and the Union. I'm speaking for you fella," he said pointing at Ciaok.

I thought, *aw naw, who's got time for this now?*

"We remain wards of the Federal government, in terms of our standing in a local or federal court," the man said. "Any suit brought would have to come from your tribe."

He again pointed to Ciaok.

"As the individuals are limited to court proceedings within the tribal government, see, due to treaty violations and collusion of all three branches of the U.S. government you legally lack sovereignty as individuals, and you lack American citizenship, unless you release your tribal membership. This here makes it nearly impossible to legally bring any such case. By the way, every inch of land that covers the United States was gotten by false premise. We know you would love to take it all back, which is why the U.S. has tried not to let you adapt, but to annihilate your people."

The man spoke as if he knew what he was rambling about.

"Good point," I said.

"You an Indian?" Ciaok cut in.

"No, but…" the stranger said.

"Well then, shut the hell up."

Both Henry and I looked at each other, and then over at the burly looking stranger, pretending to wonder to whom Ciaok meant those words, knowing fully well for whom he meant them.

"What?" the man asked, frowning as if he couldn't believe what he heard.

"Nothing," Ciaok answered, waving his hand in the air.

Whew! At the last moment he must have recalled my situation here and how vital it was for me to keep peace in this town.

Trying to restore calm, I said, "I'd only say that I measure any man by what he does as a man—good or bad."

Right then, it was Molly's voice that I heard in my head, sizing me up, "Oh, you just got no gumption, that's all," and I couldn't help but snicker.

My misplaced laugh must have appeared odd to the men sitting with me, because Ciaok and Henry, shook their heads and turned their backs to me, no longer directing talk my way. They did take back up their conversation with each other and the stranger.

Henry spoke first.

"Well, if either of you has any religion in him, according to the Old Testament, when God sent His people in to take over a land He always had them take out the original inhabitants."

Why did Henry choose to continue on that road? I thought. "Yes, but who says White men were God's people, or this was God's way," Ciaok said. "If so, then only you should follow Him," he pointed to Henry. "How could Jake or I, or even this here stranger, cause he looks nothing like you either?"

Henry studied Ciaok's face, and nodded, while I mumbled, "Don't bring me into this, now."

"Ciaok, you and he," Henry said, pointing to the stranger, "do have a point, my friend. Maybe we are all right in some ways."

"You are not my friend, Mr. Henry," Ciaok said. "I have only one White man that I trust to call me by that name. And although I like you, so far, you have not earned that right."

I was glad they left me out. I had nothing to say to add to the conversation after that, but neither did either of them.

During that moment, I thought back to a conversation I had with Alex and Ciaok before I left home. I knew why he spoke the way he did just now. I had a lot of sympathy for him, remembering how the talk ended.

That day both Alex and I had stopped talking well before the discussion was over and looked at Ciaok holding back tears in our eyes. It was in late June, almost four years ago. Spring had come and gone and summer's heat was rising. We walked on the tinder-strewn deep timbered path the last mile before emerging to walk the last quarter mile beneath the unrelenting sun near the lake. I moved closer to Ciaok and put my hand to his shoulder, gave it a squeeze, and held onto to his forearm. He shook, so I reached my arm around his back and grasped his other shoulder, feeling heavy raised scars covering his skin underneath his top.

I thought then; I was grateful that my people were not completely destroyed, and my life wasn't as difficult as his. A small part of me felt satisfaction knowing someone else was worse off than I was. I didn't like that part of me feeling that way about a good man, especially since he said his people tried to conform; still, it was not enough.

Henry and the stranger, whose name we never got, now rose to leave. Since Ciaok wasn't ready to go, we sat for a while longer. It was my day off, another reason I didn't want a scene. I played at this saloon on my off days twice a month and had to work here around these people.

"Hey Jeremiah, can I get you another drink?" The bartender asked pleasantly.

He was a pretty nice guy; treated me well, as he did most everyone in here.

"Thanks Zeke, no mo' whiskey fo' me," I said, remembering to use the dialect every so often. "I'll jus' have me a sarsaparilla and call it a day."

He turned to Ciaok.

"Anything for you?"

Ciaok was suspiciously quiet now, shaking his head at Zeke.

"After this drink," I said, "Let's get going."

Staring off into the corner of the room, he obviously wasn't done yet.

"See that there Mexican over there?" Ciaok said. "Used to be our friend, huh? Now he thinks him and the Chinaman over in the corner better than us. Yes, everyone is too good to be acquainted with the likes of you and me."

I whispered something just to settle Ciaok down and get us out of there unnoticed. I'm not sure whether I even believed what I said to him or not, but it wasn't enough.

"My friend," Ciaok said to me, "I believe there will come a day when white folks and everyone else won't ignore you and me. I call what just happened outside with Mr. Henry there, "the invisibility factor". Now, I guess we should be grateful to be ignored, if they can never acknowledge us in a way to bring us good, instead of defeat. So, I don't resent or hate anyone for being ignored by them."

Ciaok squinted his almond black eyes so hard I couldn't see the whites in them anymore.

"I said nothing about hating them. I don't hate nobody," he declared. "That's my problem. That was my great grand pappy's problem and the rest of his tribe. All my people, my papa, my grandpa, we believed their promises over and over again. Every time they broke one, we believed the next one; empty promises that turned into full-blown lies. It's because we are the ones who "didn't hate" that we are "invisible" like you. We have nothing left of what was ours—of what belonged to us."

I leaned in closer, lowered my voice and tried to lead my friend to the side door.

But, Ciaok talked even louder.

"I could name you at least five treaties that have been broken by those leaders who were supposed to be my very elected officials, too. Heck, they even stole the way we governed our tribes and used it to organize themselves."

I remember Alex telling me what he heard happened to Ciaok's family back in '27.

Ciaok went on, unable to stop himself. A few men in the room were standing up now and a couple moving our way, but he just kept going.

"Those land-hungry settlers poured into the back-country of the coastal South and began moving toward our lands. Since native tribes living there appeared to be the main obstacle to them going west, they petitioned the federal government to remove us. Ole' Presidents

Jefferson and Monroe argued that our tribes in the Southeast should exchange our land for lands west of the Mississippi River, but they did not take steps to make this happen. The first major transfer of land occurred only as the result of war. Under this kind of pressure, my people—specifically the Creek, Cherokee, Chickasaw, and Choctaw—realized that they could not defeat the Americans in war. We could not satisfy their appetite for our land. We tried to share. Give them some and hoped that if we gave up a good deal of our land, we could keep at least some part of it."

I knew what he said was true, but that would not help us now, I thought, eyeing the burly trio staring us down.

"We're supposed to be grateful that little pieces of designated Indian Territory are admitted as a part of the United States."

I laid my hand on his shoulder again, but this time he knocked it away.

"No one will listen to us," he said, pounding the table with his fist, "unless one of *them* stands up for us to tell about our lives. When we stand up for ourselves we're called aggressive and savage, no matter how much we try to be like them."

Ciaok's hands swept from his neatly combed hair, along his navy blue shirt down to his fine wool trousers.

"...to look just like them. They even took their idea of government from us, they didn't even have one, and they didn't get their model from the English or the French, either, but from us. Yet, we're still savages...ha."

"Wow, I didn't know any of this, Ciaok," I lied, then added truthfully, "I am so, so sorry this had to happen to you."

Looking around, the men in the room were ready to pounce.

"Let's go now, Ciaok!""

He stood anchored in place, unable to stop.

"We are the ones who don't deserve to be heard, cause unless they see a figure that looks like them saying it, then it's not worth their listening to or reading about."

"Ciaok, my friend," I said, "even though life has kicked you and your people in the teeth, I believe you still can find some happiness."

He didn't hear me. He was fit to be tied.

"Oh yeah, did you know one of them ole Presidents—the worst one, Jackson–didn't he do himself proud by adopting one of our children after his soldiers killed off the boy's parents? Yeah, a real hero that made him in his own bloodshot eyes, stained with the red blood of that boy's people."

"We need to go!" I exclaimed, wrenching him away now.

"Where do you think the term Trail of Tears came from? It was first used by my people, the Choctaw tribe in '32. Of the 16,000 Choctaw who walked the Trail of Tears, between 5,000 and 6,000 of us died.

I thought he would either explode or throw something across the room in a second. I was grateful the saloon was almost empty and Zeke, the bartender, liked me.

"I'm ready to go now," Ciaok said, just as the usually tolerant regulars stood directly over our table.

He may have gotten up, but was still talking, turning and placing an authoritative finger to my face as we crossed the room.

"You know the diseases my people, my great aunts, uncles, grandparents, and cousins died from when they were forced to walk all the way to Oklahoma?"

I led him three steps away from the swinging doors.

"Well, I'll tell you, they got diseases with no cures like smallpox, malaria, measles, cholera, whooping cough, influenza, and pneumonia and they died. They died with their skin falling off of their flesh."

By now, tears were pouring down his face.
"'Nunna daul Isunyi, Nunna daul Isunyi' 'Nunna daul Isunyi'," he moaned over and over again.

I held him up through the doors, hoping the outside air would release him enough to find the strength to walk the rest of the way out to the road and up the stairway to my place.

CH 15

(J)

With everything going wrong since Ciaok arrived, more than anything, I hoped I'd never see those scraggily cowhands we fought with the other day. I was grateful they were only passing through as the Illinois Central Railroad had recently added a stop near the saloon. Now that it was over, and I made it through more than 24 hours with my friend Ciaok, I needed to relax.

Times were bad but they weren't as deadly as years ago when we'd gotten hanged for fighting with those two men, no matter what the reason, lowlife bumpkins or not.

The next morning I had to get to work early. I told Ciaok to stay put and out of sight until I came back, and that was an order.

****

After I left work the next day, the aroma that met me at the back stairway was the savory smell of freshly cooked meat. Ciaok had made up something for a late supper. We spent much of the night eating and talking about old times. I'd forgotten what an excellent cookhe was for the Neuman's. At the mill, Mr. Neuman used to brag about hurrying home to eat on the cook's day off, as Ciaok added an authentic hint of hickory to the cuisine giving off a notion he was camping outdoors, instead of eating in the draperied formal dining room.

The evening shade cast shadows across the room as we sat reminiscing. The sweet, rich aroma of fresh tobacco wafted between the floorboards, drifted underneath the door and filled the room. Much better it was tonight than when there's wall to wall bodies in the saloon downstairs, when clouds of smoke rode in smothering clothes, bedding, and everything else in my room.

Some time passed before I thought to bring up Ciaok's statement he made when he first showed up here, one I didn't understand. He said Ma hadn't heard from me. She hadn't gotten any of my letters? I'd sent one...no two a long while ago to the P.O. Box for our place.

"They got nothing from you as far as I know," Ciaok said, setting the dirty plates to the side.

"But I sent the first letter well over a year ago. Maybe a year and a half."

"Man, I'm telling you they don't know where you are, if you're dead or alive. Your ma is gone off something fierce. She's not the same. And Molly didn't know anything about your going until she got back from Boston a couple of months ago, I heard."

I must have looked as if I'd seen a ghost, 'cause I felt like I'd swallowed a jackrabbit whole.

"Boston? What was Molly doing there?"

"Man, you know nothing, do you?"

In a daze, I stood up and shook my head from side to side as if it were empty and unattached to my body.

"She went there after the fire," Ciaok said, putting his hand out to steady my balance. "She's been gone almost as long as you have."

"Fire, what fire...Ma...Molly!?" I roared, losing control. I spun around and punched the tallboy in the corner of the room, hurting my fist.

"Did you just do that?" Ciaok asked, and then proceeded to tell me everything that happened after I left home that early morning, years ago, bringing up that Mr. Neuman no longer had the festivals nor allowed his wife's family to the house anymore.

I walked over to my bed and laid my head down against my bruised hand.

"Maybe after the fire and other things you say happened there, Neuman couldn't trust anybody," I cried out.

Ciaok looked down and picked up a tiny orange and black spotted insect crawling across the floor and placed it outside on the windowsill. "Maybe he can't trust them 'cause White folks know how White folks are," he said slyly.

Despite being shocked by news of the fire, and the pain in my hand, I couldn't help but snicker at Ciaok's quip.

"Not that again," I said, mildly reprimanding him, "but... yeah, who better to judge, I guess."

Ciaok picked up on my amusement, slapped his thigh, and took on his own Southern dialect; mimicking no one in particular of whom I knew.

"Yez suh, ya sho' rat there."

I was done laughing. I needed time to think about everything he'd just told me, so the rest of that night I sat and stared out the window looking for the distant horizon and nothing else.

CH 16

(J)

Two days later we returned to the SteerHouse saloon where we got into that ruckus with those two inane cowpokes. Ciaok said he needed to go back in there fora drink that the other places didn't serve; something called cactus wine. He got the drink and a wad of chewing tobacco and we were on our way out back to my place, as I had to go work in just an hour. I told Ciaok to go up to my room and get to bed early that night. I was hoping that he would be leaving in a day or two. I enjoyed his company to a point, but I'd had about enough of his snipping at everyone. We were several paces out the door, walking behind another group of men, when we were called back.

"Hey," I heard someone say, but I kept stepping.

"Hey you, not the gringos, I mean you two," someone called out. I turned around to see the Mexican "vaquero" Ciaok had been referring to in the saloon the other day, following us out of the door. I stopped just a few steps away along with Ciaok, his trousers dragging, and hair falling to the side over his eye. I was nervous– but him, no longer sorrowful and ready for a fight.

"Injun, what you look so fiery about? I didn't do nothing to you. I heard what you said. I got good ears. I can hear anything I want to hear from way across the room, if someone is talking 'bout me," he said, reaching his arm out to block our path.

I didn't want any part of this. I could fight if I needed to, but this was unnecessary. Anyway, I didn't want to blow my cover for something as worthless as Ciaok not being able to control his tongue and temper.

I could see the man's mustache-covered lips moving, but paid no attention to his words. Instead, I was busy trying to reason with him.

What could be done about Ciaok, though? He would not accept what had happened to his people. I couldn't either, but what could I do about it now?

The thick-necked man, who looked to be a miner or fur trapper, was getting more animated, so I'd thought I'd better listen to at least a little of what he was saying before he started swinging.

"We would have left you your land," he said. "We came here first; at least my distant Spanish ancestors were here first, before these now." His hand raised with a finger pointing toward the men gathered in the saloon to emphasize to whom he was referring.

Although distinctive looking, with his light beige, cattleman straw hat down-turned in the front, embroidered short leather vest, and bright red sash around his waist; the thick-necked man didn't seem so threatening now.

"When we came here, did we take everything from you? Did we send all of our people over to pretend to be your friends and then kill all of your old people and babies? Did we take your women by force?"

He then pointed to Ciaok.

"Heck, you and me, we even look alike."

Ciaok had taken on a solemn look that changed into one of a man with a renewed interest in what he was hearing.

"I'm not so sure you didn't do some of those things. I don't know everything there is to know about the past."

"'Absurdo.' You know 'mucho' about the past from what I just heard. But you can't stay there, 'amigo'. You are not living in the past, so you've got to move forward, ahead, or you will be 'loco' soon, if you are not already."

He brushed past through the doors, then stopped again, turned, and squinted at both Ciaok and me.

"I'm not your enemy, man. Hell, my country owned Texas before they took it from us," he said pointing again towards those inside the bar. "When we had it, we wouldn't let them even think about bringing slaves in there."

A huge cricket jumped along the floor between us, just outside of the hanging saloon doors. The man took time to stab it with the heavy iron spur on the back of his boot and then squish the unfortunate creature under the weight of his heel.

"If we still had that territory, and you lived there a 100 years ago and until this day," he said pointing at Ciaok, "…you would have still had your land."

"And you," he said, pointing to me, "wouldn't have ever been anything but free."

"Now, you looking like the tragic f---ing mulatto," he added, "You don't fit, so both sides treat you like s—t."

I was not sure why he added that last bit of information for me; it was Ciaok his beef was with, not me.

Ciaok looked at me and laughed, "Now there's something for you to put into your writings."

Almost done now, having had his say, the man ended the conversation by pointing to Ciaok.

"It's still worst for you, though." He said.

"So, if you looking for somebody to blame for your situation, you're looking the wrong way when you were looking at me back there, injun. Adios."

Ciaok nodded, lowering his glance to look down at the crushed insect, without saying a word. I'd thought that he might extend his arm to shake the man's out-stretched hand, but he didn't.

CH 17

(J)

Waking up the next day with a sore throat, I remembered Ma said the best thing for it was to place a pinch of salt and soda in a quarter cup of water and gargle to draw out the soreness. With the liquid swirling around my throat, the gurgling sound was loud enough to wake Ciaok who had moved during the night from sleeping across two chairs to the floor. I had to force the salty concoction down as deep as possible to get the full effect. I didn't have a moment's time to be sick.

Having talked my way out of at least one fight the night before, I could laugh about today it. Still, I had to get back some control here.

I'd planned to bring up Ciaok's leaving today.

Picking up a fountain pen and pad off my lop-sided desk strewn with papers, I planned to write up a message for him to take to Ma.

Ciaok awoke while I was writing and looked over my shoulder, reading my letter.

"Why don't you come with me instead of sending a note," Ciaok pressed.

"Ciaok, I can't leave with you now."

"Why?"

"I've got a good reason—life or death. Just take the note. I need you to take this for me."

"You know I will, anything Jake, anything."

I cringed when I heard my given name. He had to go, and quick.

"Thank you, my friend." I said, attempting to cover my anxious feelings. "I need you to deliver this message to Ma and Molly. Tell them I'm safe and I'll try to get to them as soon as I can."

"You know I will, Jake. You are good people. The best I've known since I lost my own people. I'd give my life for you, your ma, and Molly. You know that, right?" Ciaok eyes watered and his round black pupils narrowed as he went on about our years together. He seemed to know more about my past than I did. I remember Ma mentioning that she and my Pa met when they both came to Mr. Neuman's farm looking for work. I believe they fell in love rather quickly, married, and had me. I'm not so sure about what happened before they came. I got to remember to ask Ma again, when I see her. And I will see her again. I know I will.

Sun rays crept across the bed, as Ciaok rambled on, stuck in the distant past. I had to say something to bring him back to the present.

"I know, Ciaok, I've known you since I was a boy. You've always been fair, no matter what it cost you."

I stopped then, not wanting him to count what it cost him and then dwell on his ma and pa's killings.

Ciaok held out his brown, tight, weatherworn hand and put it up to his shirt pocket, pulling out a white, cotton handkerchief. He held it to his face. I waited for him.

"It's going to be alright, my friend," I offered.
I turned his attention back to the letter. "Now, Ciaok, first thing when you get home, tell Ma and Molly I'm holding up ok. And please give them this letter." I had sealed the envelope.

Ciaok carefully folded his handkerchief and placed it back into his pocket. Then he asked, "When might you be heading back? In a year, six months?"

I really was not exactly sure of how firm I was about the time period, but Ciaok seemed satisfied with it, nodding and smiling at me to confirm the statement. That was enough for me.

"I'm sure glad we met up," I said.
I knew our time together was just about over now as Ciaok paced over to the window, pulling back the curtains to look out. He stood there gazing down at the road below for a while before backing away from the chilly, biting wind seeping through one of the small cracks. He settled into a freshly dusted, brown tweed chair behind the old roll hutch desk against the side wall. I'm not sure of what had changed, but he didn't look like a man who was planning to leave the room anytime soon.

"Ahem...Ahem," I said, clearing my throat.
"Now, my friend, you've got to get going. You've got the letter now." I wasn't bucking for more trouble and

hoped he wouldn't take it the wrong way, so I continued talking in a less frustrated tone; although he sat there staring at me.

"Aye, Aye, Ciaok. You hear me good and clear, right?"

He nodded but didn't move.

"My friend," I tried to reason with him, "You know I can't have no kinda trouble here and I hate to say this, but sometimes you don't seem to care what happens to you… or maybe you do, I dunno."

Anyway, I would surely like to spend more time with you, but I just can't. You are some kind of good friend, though, that's for sure. We'll have so much more time and many more things to discuss when I get back."

I knew I had gotten through when Ciaok finally stood, raised his right arm, holding it up to his side, palm facing forward, in a traditional salute.

"God be with you," he said, "the one whom I hold out hope for." And without saying another word he slipped out through the narrow arched doorway, round the hall corner, and down the creaky, wooden, back stairs—out of sight. I looked out the side window and watched him mount his palomino. His hair flew back as he rode like the wind.

CH 18

(J)

H e was finally gone. I was glad.
I know that I'd mentioned leaving several months later, but I'd decided that this was the month I'd make my way out of this place.

I had worked every day for as many hours as I could get to save up enough money to leave Memphis and start over. Working at the saloons allowed me to hide out in a place that was not that inconspicuous. But I could think of no other way to make this kind of money–plus the men-folk had grown to appreciate the piano playing colored boy who spent all his time in a place where they met their everyday needs.

The sun was out in full force for the next four days, and given the pouring rain the last few weeks, cattlemen, miners, cowboys, and fur trappers were making their way into town for a good time.

I saw Henry again that week. He came by with a well-dressed friend to pick up where we left off in conversation about the dinner fiasco at his uncle's over a month ago. I'd tried to forget all about that evening, but Henry brought me up to date. It was still early, the saloon was empty except for the bartender and me, so I invited them around and up to my room, while I relaxed before coming back down to work later.

Henry kept right on talking as we climbed the back stairway to my door.

"I'm still not clear on what happened to the young man on the train." Henry paused and then said, "You know we are all people just the same."

Before entering my room, I took him to the side and asked who his friend was— who he'd forgotten to introduce. I wanted to remind him not to reveal my identity, which I'd shared with him just after Ciaok left. Getting back to the second part of Henry's comment, I said, "You really believe folks are all the same, but does everyone else in your family?"

He looked at me with a blank stare.

"Do all of your own people believe it?" He asked.

It didn't take me long to respond.

"They might have once, but they don't now, 'cause when they did, they got the thought beat out of them."

"Same as mine," the well-dressed friend spoke up and then followed us into my tidy room.

If I didn't know Ciaok went home, I would have thought it was him speaking, when this guest with Ciaok's same reddish brown coloring joined in the conversation.

"Yes, but who did the beating?" Henry said, taking a seat next to the bed.

Pulling out a chair for his buddy, I said, "In my case, probably the both of you."

They laughed.

Henry said, "If you want to get serious, you know I mean back before any one of us ever saw the other. The very first time White saw Red and when he first saw White. When the first Black saw the first White and vice versa. At what point do you think one put himself up as better than the other?"

The Ciaok look-alike put out his cigar in the tray on the table.

"So, it's whoever has the upper hand, wants to keep the power, anyway they can?" The other man said.

We looked hard at one another before someone spoke up.

"My people, we all still argue and fight amongst our-selves, just like I'm sure yours do," Henry said, "but when it comes to fighting outside of 'our group or regi-men' any little disagreement now becomes a major bat-tle—takes on new skirmishes and uses tactics we never resorted to before—because it always comes back to which 'regimen' is going to take control…it could be as simple as the temperature or which ice cream should be served… anything."

"Somebody always has to have the last word, huh?" the other man said, bobbing his head up and down.

"And each group thinks it must forever be someone who looks like him?" I added.

"It's for everyone's good, we truly believe this," Henry said.

"I thought it was because you felt safety in numbers, survival of fittest. It's all the same, having to always keep others under watch– keep a close eye on the ones you let in the house." I said.

"Oh, that too! You can trust no one, not really, you know?" Henry said.

"Like my old friend Ciaok, you'll recall, what he said– about you, huh?" I said.

"Guess so."

So, that's how most people think, I suspected. But for some reason, I thought Henry wasn't being truthful about his own beliefs anymore–not like at first.

"In my circle, I just sit there in the room while my aunts, uncles, cousins, and family friends go back and forth with their babble. I nod my head in agreement, adding a word here and there to let them know I'm a part of the team, on the same side. Sometimes I reveal my true hand, though, like last time." Henry said.

The pungent smell of the friend's tobacco filled my small room. I got up to open the window, but before I could take a step, a loud "thud" against the window shattered the comfortable conversation we were having inside. The window was next to the outer door leading to the back stairwell, so no one moved, suspecting that someone was outside listening.

We waited and there was another thud, then another. *Why don't they just come in and say their piece*, I thought. Henry and I crooked our necks just enough to read in the eyes of the other what he thought we should do next.

"What'd you think?" I finally asked.

"Don't know," he whispered back, heading for the door we came in, "but that door behind us is not the only way out of here."

"Well put." The other man said. "Why would you stay in a place, anyway, where someone could trap you from the outside?"

"Only problem is, I can only go out through this other door when there's no folks in the saloon downstairs. Anyways, I'd have a better chance of getting out this way," I said, pointing to the outside door, "if I could get past the person, and end up outside in the open. When I did, leastways, I'm not still cooped up inside of a building after making my escape from this room."

Henry shook his head and offered up a belly laugh.

"Don't know how, but that makes some kinda' sense," he said.

"We have to make a move now, after that noise you just made, Henry," the other man said.

"Ok, let's go. You first," I said.

Taking the challenge, the man stood up and backed over to the corner of the room next to the door and went out the way we came in. Henry followed. I shut and locked the door behind us.

******

I wasn't surprised when Henry stopped into the saloon the next day before I began playing, and took me to the side.

"Jake," he said.

I looked around before I could stop myself, then tried to pretend that it was a coincidence and I was looking for something.

"I'm sorry it slipped." He said.

I looked down and refused to look up at him, as he spoke to me in a whisper.

"No one's nearby. We both know I know who you are and why you changed your name, and I don't believe you are guilty of anything."

Could I trust anyone? A friend was someone you could trust with all your feelings. But should you trust anyone with your life? Maybe I should have listened to Ciaok and kept my mouth shut.

"I will keep calling you Jeremiah, I promise, but I can't help you unless you share everything with me."

How could Henry help me? He may be White, and he may be a fair man, but those men who may have killed Ezra probably were still looking for me and they were anything but fair.

"Mr. Henry, can I play something for you?" I said, loudly for the men at the bar staring.

As Henry shouted his response, more inquiring eyes turned in our direction.

"Sure, play Dixieland for me, Jeremiah, my boy."

He patted me on the back and went back to the counter to place his order.

The sun wasn't beaming so much as I remembered, when I woke up earlier that morning.

CH 19

(J)

A few days later, I went out to get some chewing tobacco to take up a new habit. I'd gotten the idea watching Ciaok and hoped it would make me even more believable as Jeremiah.

That was when Henry walked past me, without a word. I knew the protocol and played along. He didn't know me. Knowing me would make him seem lowly to his friends and to the gentlemen and ladies walking nearby. Why, his folks might even get wind of it. I almost laughed thinking of their reaction. Again I wondered, could I trust him with my secret?

I remembered it was coming around to harvest time at home, so I took off some time to venture outside of the few blocks that made up the town center to consider how people do things around here. On the last block, riding along side was a tired, dusty horse pulling an empty old wagon with a miner at the helm. It had almost creaked past, before falling into a ditch and splattering the muddy remnants from last night's rains, all over my grey trousers. Cursing under my breath, I stepped up to the horse trough, dipping my hat in a few times for water to wash them and let them dry with the afternoon sun.

Once out of town, I walked past a mixed scene of celebrations, like the ones I'd witnessed at home in Grenada—there were sharecroppers and children bobbing for apples.

At one place, where strangely everyone was very white-skinned with carrot, red hair, the family sat outside on the porch playing a fortune-telling game using colorful saucers. On the farms further out, many of the adults and some children resembled Ciaok. One little boy, with shoulder length black hair pulled into two twisted plaits, acknowledged my presence with a regal head nod. I thought he may have descended from a chieftain and wondered why he was living in that sectioned off space which didn't match the stories he was told of his grandfather. I turned and walked down a road past families of Negro sharecroppers. I saw a small framed grandmother-type, rocking back and forth, her head raised and eyes squinting into the sunset behind me. I edged closer and moved into her view. She looked at me, then looked away without acknowledging my hand raised in respect for her presence.

From inside came two small boys and a young girl. The children stepped down onto the worn, splintered wooden floor boards, past the woman in the rocking chair, then to the dirt and tiny rock covering on the ground below. Following behind them was a bespectacled man, I would take to be their father and the old women's son. He stopped short, sitting down on one of the two step boards, reached underneath, and took out a long loose board from under the stairs.

"Evening sir," I said, trying to show him I meant no harm.

He didn't speak.

I'd only offered a quick, polite greeting. I thought, what was the problem? As I backed away, the man uttered, "What'd you wont?"

I really hadn't stopped, nor slowed my stride. I gave only a casual, neighborly gesture as I passed by. I was not sure why he asked me this; I hadn't come to his ramshackle place to pay anyone a visit.

"Just walking by," I said. The old women, now moved and picked up her cane from beside her rocker.

"What reason you got for that?" the man asked me. I wanted to say to him, "*I'm like you. I'm just passing through this time and place.*" But can't a man just walk by? I wondered.

"You reckon you sumpin,' cause you got time to jus' walk 'round doing nuthin,' " he said.

I had to say something, but didn't know how to say it. Then someone spoke for me.

"Howdy!"

One of the young boys had come around behind me, while I focused on what the man would say next.

"Mister, why is yo' britches all wet-looking?" the boy asked.

I chuckled, and extended my hand, "Hello, and what's your name?"

"I'm Caleb."

The boy began fingering the emblem of a horse attached to the chain hanging from my pocket.

"Do you like horses, Caleb?

"We don't have no horses. I see them riding by… I do, and I sho' would like to touch me one."

"I liked horses when I was a boy, too. I used to ride one that the owner of the land I lived on had especially for me." I exaggerated a bit.

The boy's eyes widened 'til his tiny brown irises reflected the fading sunlight.

"Fo' sho'?"

"Yes, I did. And if you ever get to town up there," I said, pointing in its direction, "ask for me, Jeremiah. I will see if I can get a horse you can do more than just touch."

The boy gazed over at his grandfather and the older lady on the porch.

By now, the old woman had laid her cane back down on the wooden floor and the man had let go of the board he was holding.

I waved at them one more time and kept walking, and this time they both waved back.

By the time I passed that last shanty in view, the sun had already disappeared behind the raised, sloping land ahead. I rounded one of the tall, leafy oaks and stepped onto the dusty road back to town.

****

I seemed to avoid Henry all the time now that he had slipped and mentioned my name in the saloon. Or maybe he's avoiding *me*. If so, I'm glad. It could be my imagination, but it seems like he looks right through me and sees my soul. I should ask him how he found out more than I'd told him, but I don't even care. I just hope he keeps quiet and can be trusted not to go to the sheriff.

"Speak of the devil!" I remarked when Henry sneaked through the closed back door of the saloon that morning. He asked me to follow him over to a discreet side booth near the back.

"Jeremiah, yes, I know a little more about who you are. But, you don't have to be afraid. I've noticed that you purposely don't make yourself available to talk anymore. I'd like to help you in any way I can. Will you please talk to me?"

"Why—we're talking now, Mr. Henry, ain't we?"

I added the "Mr." and the "ain't" because someone with his ear cocked came in and passed near the table where we were sitting. But maybe I should from now on, I thought.

"Jeremiah," he whispered, "Why don't you trust me anymore? If you will listen, can I tell you what I see when I observe you?"

I knew it.

"Go ahead." I whispered, "Who are you, anyway? Some kind of head doctor?"

He chuckled, then went on, "I believe you have descended from a long line of people, on both sides, who have been held back through no fault of their own. They have been led to believe that they cannot accomplish something major—no matter what their dreams. Still, you set goals, because you wish to be more than what you are. Then you delay, and delay and delay, why? Although you want better- you even dream big- deep down you haven't fiery drive because those before you haven't modeled it. They were robbed of the opportunity you have. There is no view from your past to make your striving more than just a dream, but a true reality.

"You write down what you feel because you can't trust what will happen if you say what you're thinking to the people in your life. You fear they will laugh at you, ostracize you, or worse, won't accept the man that you are. Your thoughts and your feelings are real. They have value not just for you, but for anyone who listens."

After listening to Henry, I thought he made sense and maybe I could trust him.

"You know, it's funny that you tell me this, because I had another dream the other night. I don't know what to make of it, but it was strange.

"In the dream, *I was sitting on a tree stump outside near the saloon, when it suddenly became the house I grew up in. As I looked at the side of the house, I saw a mama duck, then her baby ducks, go through a tiny little opening under the house. I ran over to see how they got in, 'cause I didn't know of any opening large enough for a family of ducks to fit through and expected to see them inside wreaking the room.*

"But the opening turned into an underground cellar or hidden porch underneath the house. The ducks turned into dogs. Black, long-haired dogs, like the one I always was asking my ma and pa for when I was a kid. She cradled her ducklings, now pups. One pup came out and my sister ran out of the saloon, which had turned into my childhood home. 'I can't help it. I'm go- ing to give it something to eat.' She said. 'Anything. It's starving. Poor little 'ting.' She went in and came out with a chunk of meat, soft candy, and some bacon grease

with corn pone. Each time she dropped anything, the pups would devour it. The last chunk he picked up and took back underneath the house to the hidden cellar or porch. "We'll never get rid of them now," I said. "They will be scratching at our door forever." The pup grew up right there and became a little boy with curly black hair. He was healthy, happy and one of the family. Any thought of never having him in the midst of us was one we could never have fathomed."

Finished, I paused for breath and looked at Henry.

"Hmm... I could be a head doctor," he said.

"But I'm no dream weaver. Maybe it has something to do with you and your own metamorphosis. Taking on responsibilities of someone else you never wanted to, someone you couldn't imagine a life without and you've lost."

"Dunno...could be." I shrugged and then slid off the long hard bench to finish up my noon shift.

"Well, I don't know either. Like I said, I'm no dream weaver, so no more about your convoluted night-mares...ok?" Henry laughed, moving towards the front— putting some distance between us.

CH 20

(J)

She looked to be about 23 years old when I first saw her. A friend, I guess you could say I would have liked to call her that. She slid past the swinging doors of the saloon, black as opal. Was she the new owner, Mr. Oliver's secret woman? I wondered. She was giving orders and commanding girls, of every shade and hue.

"You go with that one," the young woman told one girl. She was running the place like a madam, a term new to my vocabulary.

Her marble-smooth skin and slim, striking frame demanded attention and respect. Her hair was thick, black and velvety, with tightly coiled curls and twists on top. It made her look queenly and statuesque.

I never expected that she like me—would try to hide from something or someone, but I knew right at that moment, I loved her.

"Good morning."' she said.

When she smiled, her teeth shone porcelain white resting between full, plum-colored lips. Her onyx skin, tight across her high cheekbones, seemed to caress her oval face. When she opened her mouth to speak, she lightly smacked her lips unconsciously.

There was a little boy standing outside, with his back to the swinging doors, waiting for her.

I didn't get to see her as often as I would have liked. It would be another two months before I saw her again. I had no idea why she came in the saloon only once since I'd arrived. I wasn't sure, and I didn't care. I looked for her to come through the doors each day until I saw her again, because I knew there was something strange and different about her, and I was drawn to whatever it was.

Chapter 21

(*M*)olly

One rainy, afternoon in April, three months after I'd returned home from Boston, the postmaster in Misterton sent word to Ma that there was a small package with her name written on all four sides. It sat on the edge of a side table in back of the post office with no return address.

"Enola, here it is." The postmaster pointed.

He moved behind the counter to the back of the room and picked up what looked like an eight square inch box off of the table.

"To be so tiny, it's heavy," he said, "makes me feel like an ox luggin' a plow, it does."

I took hold of one corner and he had the other.

It wasn't all that heavy for one person. I think the postmaster was trying to be amusing.

As there was no return name on it, which made it even more mysterious, I opened the box there. There was unnecessary packing inside it that weighed it down, so I threw that out. Inside the box was just a letter.

I came to the front counter with the strange package, took out the letter which was missing an outside envelope, and handed it over to Ma. As we sat down together to read it, we noticed the date on the first and only page—March 1880— which was over a year ago.

March 11, 1880
Dear Ma,

I know Molly is off somewhere giving Alex a hard time. I know she turned everyone's heads at the Autumn Festival last year. Tell her I hated that I didn't stay long enough to see her that day, but I had to go. There will be other Autumn Festivals and I'll be there to see her and Alex and hopefully their young'uns one day. I cannot tell you why I have not written before now. But you know I would have if I could. I still plan to go north, but have not made it all the way just yet. I am surviving, that's all I can say for now. You can't write to me, Ma. I don't know if I will be here for much longer. I will write you and Molly again when I can.

Love,
  J

Stunned, the letter tumbled from Ma's hands to the floor. I reached down to pick it up. We both jumped up and then Ma grabbed my arm and pulled me close.

"Molly, this letter is dated over a year ago. I do know a year is a long time, but the date was after I went up to Hardeman. Yes, it is."

"I don't know Ma, this letter is from a long time ago. Even if the poor soul they brought back from the woods wasn't Jake, it's hard to hope just from this. Why did it take so long to get to us, and why hasn't Jake come home since? Even if he kept going north and got established, he wouldn't just forget us, would he, Ma?"

Once more, I sat down on one of the chairs alongside the window. Ma slipped over and sat next to me, placing her head in her hands.

We had too many questions that neither one of us could answer. I think I had finally accepted that Jake was probably gone. And although it was hard, Ma had done the same. We didn't want to hope and die inside all over again. I didn't think Ma could live through it one more time.

With his eyes downcast, the postmaster had long stopped trying to make us laugh. Ma and I got up, nodded respectfully to him, then drifted out the door with our heads bowed and letter in hand.

Chapter 22

(J)ake

I'm almost asleep, now….57…56….

I could hear Ma talking to Molly in the kitchen. I was back home, somehow. I could hear her voice so clearly. Everything before must have been a dream. I got out of my bed and came out to the front room.

"Morning Ma, what's to eat? M--a?"

Why didn't she turn around towards me?

"Ma, I say, what's for breakfast?

"I hope Molly didn't make it."

I figured early morning was as good a time as any to get at my sister, before she started in on me, but even she didn't respond. I rushed over and stood between them. But it was like they didn't see me. Then Ma began talking to Molly as if I wasn't even in the room or anywhere around.

153

"I saw a man that looked like a preacher. He was praying over Jake." Ma said to Molly. "He was telling the preacher he was already saved, laying with his back against the ground, but the preacher was still praying and casting. Then the preacher was gone and three people, don't know who they are, but I can see them looking below through a drop down window over the door."

"Ma… Ma. Listen to me! I'm here, Ma!" I hollered.

Then I woke up.

It was another nightmare. Heck, I needed to get some sleep. I turned over and counted back: 100, 99, 98, 97, 96, 95…

I remember the first time Ma heard me "number- ing," I was in the bed, awake for going on an hour, when she came in to check on me. My feet barely made it down past the middle of the bed then.

"Why you still awake?" Ma wanted to know.

I tried to quickly shut my eyes, hoping it might fool her, but it didn't work.

"I can't get to sleep Ma."

She held her hand to my forehead.

"Do you feel sick?"

I instinctively pulled my hand up over the cover to rest on my stomach.

"If you feel sick there, and don't want me to look, I can call your Pa in here to check on you."

My hand immediately dropped back down to my side. "No Ma, it's nothing, nothing like that where you need to wake Pa."

I twisted and turned onto my side to let her know I was ready to get about the business of trying to bring on my nighttime slumber.

"Well then, son, you'd best get some rest."

"I'm trying. I started over tonight, after I got all the way to 1. That's so different, cause I'm usually asleep 'fore then," I said.

"I don't have a notion what you're getting at, but I will get back in here and check on you again in about 30 minutes."

"Okay Ma," I moaned.

When I woke up, it was the next morning. I figure I fell asleep by the time Ma came back in to check on me.

✳✳✳✳✳✳✳✳

I can't even sleep anymore. It hits me every night. Thinking about what was, Ma and Molly, and what I want to do. When I do sleep, I dream I am back home, living a strange existence where no one can see me. But I'm not at home, and this place is the only one I have right now.

I pulled up the covers, feeling an icy breeze coming through the shutters. Well—a few more weeks here won't matter. I can take it. It's better than the alternative, the one I don't want to face up to. It's the other reason I had to leave that day. I couldn't take it anymore.

Would anyone believe me? If anybody listened, they'd think I was writing some flowery lines for the piano for that pretty girl who worked at the Freedman's store back home.

I recall the first time Molly and Ma saw some of my 'thinking' put to paper. It was around the time I was beginning to get good at it.

"Why don't you be a writer?" Molly said.

"And?" I asked

"Be one of those people who makes sort of a living writing in those newspapers or even a book or something."

"Why would I do something like that?"

"Cause you seem to be somewhat good at it, based on the little part I've seen. I hate to say."

"Don't you know those people do all the work and get none of the recognition? Those other one's who take the writings and put it on the stage as reenactments or plays, they get all the respect and attention.

"But, I would figure that's what you would want—not to be seen or heard from." she said.

"Okay, you're right, I don't want all that attention, but I do want some decent pay for all the time and work it takes to write down something that's worth reading."

"Oh, I thought you did it out of the utter joy of not having to talk to anyone while you're doing it."

Not giving into another second of her nonsense, I shook my head at her silliness and then got up to leave, shoving her to one side on my way out the door. But I wasn't angry then; I could never get too upset with her.

CH 23

(J)

The sun was coming straight through the missing slat in one of the shutters. The sunlight was pushing me to get moving, but I was too tired to budge.

I laid there and thought about the life I had back then. So much had happened in the South, in such a shortperiod of time, to change the way Negros lives were supposed to be lived. Most changes were for the better, but some things seemed almost no different than what I remember as a little fella. It could be that I don't remember some happenings and may have heard about them from older folks or reading from torn history books in Mr. Temple's class. I always did like him more than any of my other schoolhouse teachers. Most of them were usually womenfolk.

Not that I had anything against womenfolk, but it's just that Mr. Temple was able to get us books, albeit weatherworn, they gave us a window into what had happened in the world. He also got us copies of *The Colored Citizen* out of Vicksburg and other current newspaper publications from the North and this part of the South; Mr. Temple believed that we should know more than just reading, writing, and arithmetic. He would travel to Vicksburg on his day off to get *The Citizen* and *The Baptist Signal*. Then Mr. Temple took out a subscription and would pick up the papers from the postmaster in Misterton after he found that it would be safe to do so.

However, it didn't seem like things had changed much since my early childhood. Some things I remembered, I wanted to forget. By the time I could attend school and learned to read, I found out why life was even harder back then compared to now.

When I was eight years old, Congress passed The Civil Rights Act, in April 1866. It was the first federal law that was supposed to protect the rights of Negros. President Andrew Johnson vetoed it, but Congress overrode the veto.

That same year, in November, the final Congressional elections of the year and election of additional Republicans lead to southern Reconstruction being taken over by the federal government and Freedman's rights backed. Ma had said that was a great day.

But the year wasn't over yet, when I remember hearing Pa read in *The Colored Citizen* on Christmas Eve that some people called the Klu Klux Klan formed secretly to discourage Negros from voting in a brutal and shameful way to take away our civil rights we'd only just gotten.

I'd asked Ma about them once and she said the Klan was Mississippi's response–after the Civil–to Reconstruction. Whites hated the new South and retaliated because freed slaves could now go to school and become owners of farms and businesses.

We were in the middle of Reconstruction now, or we're supposed to be, but businesses like ole' Mr. Richmond's mercantile back home were fighting the reconstruction efforts with every inch of their being.

About the time Reconstruction began, I was about six or seven and a few years later life changed. It was the last time I remember seeing Pa. I always believed that the Klu Klux Klan had something to do with his going away.

****

"Ahh, got to get up."

Get cleaned, all ready to make it through another day in hiding.

Before swinging my legs over to the floor, I stretched my arms and extended my back until it cracked.

"Boy, you're going to make it," I told myself this morning.

I keep telling myself this as I reached for the half-filled glass water jug to empty into my metal wash basin, before heading for the place outside to empty it or relieve myself.

My last chore before heading downstairs was to latch on to the thick braided rope hanging from the oversized slat in the middle of the ceiling. It was looped up and draped to the side with the knotted end resting on top of the seven-foot highboy pushed up against the wall in the farthest corner of the room. The chest was high enough, so no one who might happen to come in would see the rope pulled across the room. Though it resembled a noose, I kept it there, atop of the highboy, to stretch out my back and chest muscles, and to keep my tired arms from getting stiff.

I finished my morning routine early and then slipped downstairs, to look in on the saloon. I made certain no one saw me use the inside staircase.

As my boot stuck on one, then the next creaking step, I recalled what happened after the last time I tried the same thing about five months ago. I had needed a second log to warm my room, so I made the mistake of shamelessly accessing the saloon using this same stairway. I thought I might get what I needed from next to the huge wood-burning stove that warmed the establishment during those colder winter months.

"Hey there boy, what in the tarnation do you think yo' doing in here by yo' self?" the owner said, emerging from a tiny, curtain-covered room behind the counter.

I didn't dare remind him he hadn't minded the first time he caught me down here, since it has benefited his saloon, especially since I'd started "stroking those keys" as he called it.

"Boy, get this and get it now! The only reason all these White folks let you sit in here without hurting yo' is 'cause you play that there piano. Hell, we even let you come through those front swinging doors."

I stood with my hands to my side, not moving an inch, waiting until he finished his tirade.

"Freedman Bureau, Reconstruction or not, you better not ever let me catch you in here alone again. Ya' hear."

"Yes, suh. Never again," I said.
By now, the new owner had been here three months, and I knew his routine. He wouldn't be back here for another week, and the bartender for another hour. I would be long gone by then.

I had been the official caretaker and piano player for the saloon since the first week after I'd arrived in town. At this moment, as I emerged from the last step into the dining room, I imagined I could hear my customary song playing in the back corner of the room. This piece had been requested by cowboys, fur trappers, miners, gamblers and everyone else who came through the swinging doors–even the dancing girls they tried to impress. True, I hated the visions this song conjured up, but years ago, when I'd first learned 'Dixie, it was the favorite of ex-President Abraham Lincoln–so I spent a whole summer perfecting it. Whenever I got time off at the mill, I would follow Ma to the Neuman's parlor to practice.

The song played over and over in my head.

"I wish I were in Dixie, hooray, hooray, in Dixie land I'll take my stand to live and die in Dixie,"
"Away, Away, away down south in Dixie."

"Wait a second," I said to myself. "Did I really hear music?"

Looking around for what or who I didn't know, 'cause I hadn't been sure of anything for a mighty long time. Before I strode closer to that side of the room and locked my eyes on the back of the piano, from here it looked to be playing by itself—with no fingers spread atop the black and white keys.

Abruptly, the sounds coming from that music box changed from "Dixie" to every lyrical note I'd hoped I'd written. It was a living thing, heard only by me. I envisioned my words, feelings, the reason for being, all on display. Not the endless parade of numbers that filled my head when I worked at the mill, but the hidden illuminating visions that flow through my mind constantly. The floor planks beneath my worn rawhide boots rang poetic with a raised circular pattern like a photograph I'd seen of a Roman coliseum in Mr. Temple's class years ago. The stone edifice on paper was a round, never-ending maze with grassy brown earth in the middle where men fought wild animals and each other for their lives.

I stepped on one board, then the next, as I moved closer to the sound coming from across the room. I was mesmerized, yet fearful, at the same time.

"Phew," I sighed, wiping my brow with the back of my hand. At the piano sat a woman…playing passionately. Her lovely head barely rose above the top of the piano's tall, brown raised back. *It was her.*

Raven-colored hair and a dress that was equally dark, she blended into the décor. Another reason I gave myself for not noticing her outline moving over the black and white keys. Her thick mane hung in a twisted plait on the left side of her face. It flowed past her shoulder and rested just above her gleaming deep brown skin on her visible upper chest. The top of the piano hid a lemon sash tied just above her waist, accentuating her sleek, delicate outline. I'd never seen anyone like her since that first day she came through the swinging doors of the saloon. Her perfect frame, almost the color of her hair, resembled a jaguar–keen and sinewy. The fear of approaching such a fine specimen with an obvious musical flair–her fingers still gliding over the keyboard and slim feet pressing against the pedals–was overshadowed by the greater knowledge that I could only appeal to her as a lesser artist.

How could this be only my second time seeing her? The first time, when she came through the swinging doors of the saloon one night, two months ago, leaving a little boy standing outside. I was sure I would have seen her again before now. Maybe I should approach this musical prodigy directly——as her potential pupil. If that's the only way I could get to talk to this majestic, midnight nymphet——then so be it.

I wish I'd gotten up my nerve quicker, as the sound of customers gathering outside early prompted me to dart up the stairs as she jumped and shot out the back door. The owner had made it clear once before. Only when there were paying customers, or during my allotted time to practice, was I to be down there. At no other time were people like us——this prodigy and me——to be unchaperoned down in the saloon dining area. Every time I deigned to sneak in there on my own, it was at my own risk. I'm sure it was the same for her. I didn't see her in there again after that second time.

CH 24

(J)

Back upstairs, I thought about an earlier conversation with Ciaok. At first, I'd told him, I had no plans to share my real identity with Henry. However, I changed my mind just after Ciaok left and then learned that Henry had already found out a lot on his own.

"*You said you weren't, now what'd you want to tell him who you are for?*" I could hear him say.

Although Ciaok made me nervous, being able to talk every day to someone who knew me made a difference. I couldn't explain just how good it felt having at least one person knowing the real me. I figured, like any other human being, I just needed someone to talk to.

Ciaok had said. "But you know why you can't trust no one. Why you gonna trust folks when they can't even trust themselves? They say they're gonna do one thing and then their insides tells them to do another. How you gonna put yourself in their confidence?"

"It's just that I would like someone," I said at first.

"Humph, folks don't even know what they're gonna do from one day to the next. They'll never tell you that, though. You looking at them from the outside going, 'I 'spect I can trust this fella to help me through this, I... humph...'"

When Ciaok stood up and kicked his boot heel against the bed's brown, scratched railing, I knew not to try to stop him from saying his piece.

"You can trust 'em...you can trust 'em alright... that they gonna do something that's gonna make you lose all that faith you had in 'em. That's what they're gonna do, I tell ya."

He'd sat back down and left a moment open for me to speak. The room was getting colder with the flames dying down.

"That's something else, you're talking about." I said. "I know that life's happenings change folks and some-times the good they intend to do, they don't."

He'd walked over and poked at the embers, while I continued talking.

"Ciaok, you're talking about those folks who are lis-tening to you and saying they understand and want to help you. All the while they're looking at you, but know they're your enemy. They're not a friend who's just a little envious," I'd said. "Shoot, we know that happens all the time. But someone like that... they're a real, mean varmint. They never cared for you or most of the people they pretend to care for- like the jackal they are— with no feelings, no regrets, and no conscience."

Ciaok had nodded in agreement, putting the poker back in its holder.

"But, most people aren't that way," I told him. "Don't you think I've got to take a chance and confide in a man who has shown for the last several months that I can trust him with my secret?"

I remember Ciaok sat down and pulled a dingy, gray kerchief from his shirt pocket. He wiped his nose while shaking his head. He then turned and stared at the smoldering embers in the small wood-burning stove across from the highboy. Finally, he took his time stuffing the kerchief back, looked up and pointed his finger at me like a six-shooter, proclaiming, "You're nuts."

******

The stars were out that night. But I didn't dream; it was more like a nightmare. Maybe it was the late night meal, 'cause I had a hard time getting to sleep. There was a full moon out and hundreds of tiny stars were clearly visible from my unshuttered window. A blanket of deep blue darkness with speckled pinpoints lit up the sky. I laid in bed with my eyes open counting down for the second time and was now almost sleep... 37, 36, 35...

The saloon "lent" me out to play for a gathering of some sort in a huge auditorium. The coach came in from some town outside of Memphis, maybe Nashville. I met up with a family traveling, I'd known them for years. We were inside a big open hall where this convention of some sort was going on. They were auctioning off rich folks' possessions on one side of a brown, paneled wide-open room and in another smaller white- washed room on the other side. There was a third room where people were eating and drinking, but it was men, women, and children—entire families. Outdoors, there was an open area surrounding the great hall, all grassy with paths cut through to other smaller buildings with stairs and paneled glass windows throughout. Inside, I discussed my current situation, since they knew me, and told them I was heading back home for the holidays. There were dark clouds hanging low—almost touching the treetops, with many horses and coaches of the well-to-do hitched to posts or set down in rows to the back.

"Would you look at that?" I heard someone say when I saw the first drops fall. The man speaking was definitely one of those that was more than nearly well off. He had on long tailcoat and an ascot in place of a tie.

"I think we are going to get some rain," he said, looking out of one of the glass doors.

When I looked back at what I'd already heard a few minutes earlier, I knew we were in trouble. The well- dressed man's voice rose as if he wanted to compete with the thundering booms outside.

"Could the buckets of water drop any faster and harder than that torrential downpour out there?" He shouted, pointing to houses that looked like they were on the verge of being washed away. I could see them through the glass partitions leading out.

People were being motioned to run out the side door on the other side of the hall to higher ground, as the water got so deep on the one side it rose two to three inches against the entrance doors. The liquid poured through when an agitated, older women holding a tiny dog tried to get out on that side. The dapper gentleman I'd been speaking with was now running in circles and screaming.

"I have to... I have to find them. Where are they?"

I didn't waste precious time telling this man, who had turned from me to scourer the room for his wife and two children, that I was heading for higher ground on the other side of the great hall myself. By now, the water was bursting through the front entrance doors.

I pushed through the crowd, racing to the south door with the throngs of bodies knocking one another down to squeeze past me. On the other side of the building, on the outside, the once grassy land had turned to waves rising higher and higher before plateauing on the steep- est point near two small buildings that sat northeast and west from the one we were now trying to escape. The scores of people–already out, drenching wet, and swimming through the water–were making their way to the smaller reddish brown brick structures that were built exactly like the great brick hall we'd just left. By the time I reached that other building on the northwest side, I turned and looked down towards the great hall hoping to see that family behind me or at least emerging from the inside.

Eventually, the rain slowed to a drizzle and all that was left was...

Well, let me put it this way: the rain lasted only 30 minutes and instead of the high ground, the land before me now looked to be a flooded low-lying valley with a river rippling through it.

Amid all the commotion, men, women and children clutched each other and cried. Witnessing all of this sadness and the shimmering rush of water, how could I not long for my family—to be home with them.

Then, in front of me, to the east, and to the west, a smoky haze stretched out beyond the horizon, where my range of vision ended—it carried on. Through the misty clearing, the sun burst forth strangely, exposing limbs. Faces, armor, weapons, lace, and headpieces were laid bare. They were more than just images I saw labeled past, present and future—they were living things reaching out to me.

I fixated on one scene, a glistening figure of a small framed woman, watching her children battle in front of her. The brownish-red blood oozing down from wounds in their little chests. Was that their mother? What were they fighting over? Something that wasn't even theirs yet—that still belonged to her? The woman's eyes were sad, filled with tears and mourning, a   sea of regret spilling onto the landscape. But still she was grabbing, clutching for more, same as the young one's she cried for.

Smiles, grimaces, fists, and legs tangled around torsos, mud-covered, all moving in stone-baked, brown pewter. Eyes fierce, ready to grasp at something to escape alive.

But no one did. None of them. Each one struggled for that something. What? The sun, strange, ominous, bouncing off the edifice decreed, "It's over."

Explosions overhead, like omens proclaiming the end of something. Was it greed, yearning, envy, strife, longing? Everyone and everything—gone.

Where had they gone? I asked.

A voice said, "They were told it would end."

The distant haze clearly hovering over the endless shining alloy made me dizzy. My eyes moved from one end of the earth to the other.

They lived, battled and lost.

I knew it.

Had I lost? I asked.

So many did.

I couldn't look up again.

From far above, I could hear a different voice, it sounded like a woman, like Ma.

"Molly and now you. My children's always dreaming of something other than what they already got. You can't live long that way. Got to be grateful for what you got...the rest will come."

Then, in front of me, I saw Molly. She was walking back from the woods on the other side of Milcreek Pond. I said something to her, and I didn't realize it was me speaking. I thought it was Ma or anyone else, but me.

"What?" My sister said.

I turned to face her and said, "If you live in the past, while grabbing for the future, then your present will pass you by."

I woke up shaking and stared out the window. It was still dark outside. I couldn't get back to sleep for most of the night.

CH 25

(J)

The next morning, with last night's images still running through my head, I could barely think about work that day. I wasn't sure what it all meant or if it meant anything at all. What I did know was that before going down to work that afternoon, I had to get away from these four walls and breathe in some fresh morning air.

I took a stroll to clear my mind out into the less rugged countryside, like the one I'd taken when I first came to town.

I didn't feel like putting on an act that morning for anyone who thought they knew me.

Walking down the rocky, dirt road, seeing the mixture of neatly kept and rundown shanties from before, I stopped in front of that one particular house again, as I did on the last trip. This time, I'd thought it was abandoned, until I saw the old women, as before, rocking on the porch. Of all the houses I'd seen on my excursions just outside of town, it needed the most work.

Standing on the ramshackle porch was a bent-over old man talking loudly to the gray-haired woman gently swaying back and forth.

As I moved past, that's when *she* walked out from behind the patched door.

We recognized one another right away.

It surprised me when she waved, as if she'd accepted my invitation to come courting or something. I raised my arm, a move that prompted the old man to spit, then glare, as if warning me I had better not.

That's when the graceful young woman stepped off of the porch and glided towards me. She stopped in the middle of the road.

"I see's we meets again." She said, smiling that gleaming white grin of hers.

"Um… yes…um…my name's Jeremiah."

"I's Telma."

"Howdy, Telma." I held my hand out.

Standing behind her was the small boy I'd spied waiting for her outside the doors of the saloon. He stepped out from behind the open door onto the creaky wooden porch and came over to stand next to Telma. All the while, he never took his eyes off of me.

She lifted her hand above her brow, squinting from the glare of the sun, then placed her fingers on the boy's head.

I realized this was the boy I talked with on my first excursion out-of-town months earlier.

"This's my boy, Caleb. He's pa is dead."

I hadn't asked her, but I guess she must have read my interest, and figured I should know the details.

""They shot him in the back," she added, "Oh, 'bout six or seven years ago. Caleb here, was only a babe when it happened."

I tried to look as sorrowful as I could at her revelation, as she placed her hand on her son's head.

"The sheriff, he said, that Caleb's pa was trying to steal something outside that there SteerHouse saloon and a gambler killed him fo' good reason. Wasn't nothing we could say or do 'bout it."

I felt anger rising in me and I didn't have to create the look of fury on my face.

"That's my ma and pa on the porch there. My brother and his two kids were over fo' a few weeks, but they since gone home. "We," Telma said, pointing to herself and then to Caleb, "still living with my folks. Never did git the chance to move away and 'fore long my man was gone."

When she stopped to take a breath, I took notice of the long green and white, stripped two-piece outfit. It flattered her figure even more.

"You don't say much, do you?" I said, trying to make the conversation lighter.

"You either," she said, perceptively noting I had given her nothing more to go by than my 'made-up' name.

"Tell me more about Telma," I said, determined not to reveal any details about myself.

"Ain't much more to tell." she began.

"I used to be one of the girls who come to dance with the men, then get 'em to buy drinks. The men pay regular price for my drink, but I's really served cold tea or colored water. The extra money left over was split twixt me and the owner. I was making enough to take care of myself and my boy and even help my ma and pa, but I had's to go 'cause they kept trying to git me to do more than just dance. I wasn't gonna have none of that."

I didn't know what to say to her after that, but, "How did you learn to play the piano like I heard that day at the saloon?"

"Can't say how. No one taught me. It was like I always knew. I sat down one day when I first saw one when I ended up in a saloon—at first to clean.   I been playing ever since—any chance I gits."

"So what are you doing now?"

"Well, I reckon, most saloons don't wont no female playing piano for they's customers, so I'z trying to find work as a maid or caring for some rich folks chil'ren. That way I leastways can git to play again sometimes– by myself. But rich folks ain't plentiful enough these days, and I can't keep up this place, now lately my boy don't wanna talk no more."

Telma's little boy was humming and running in a circle around us, when her father stepped off the porch and started walking up on us. By then, I knew it was time to get on, as the sun was further away, barely peeking through a sky littered with clouds.

"I hope we meet again soon, Telma, and that you get the work you need."

"Thanks. Bye, Mr. Jeremiah."

The rest of the way home I thought about that stripped suit, and how it hugged her frame. I went to sleep that night with Telma on my mind.

CH 26

(J)

On Saturday, I was playing piano in my regular saloon when the sheriff came in peering from table to table, then from one corner of the bar to the other. My fingers stiffened causing me to miss a key, wondering what he wanted here, and if I was right to trust Henry?

The Memphis lawman had come in maybe once or twice this past week and sat down next to Henry's Uncle Matthew, whom I'd spied slinking in. I didn't think he'd recognized me or even looked my way. I made a point to stare straight ahead, embracing the keys in front of me when either of them came in. This afternoon, out of the side of one eye, I saw Henry's uncle walking over to the counter and ordering a whiskey before he went back to the table. The men spoke a good while, before the sheriff rose from the table, looked over towards me and bolted through the swaying doors.

It was time for me to get out of there now. I knew it. Something was going on. I had almost decided to make my way out of Memphis just the week before, and I was not sure how, but I was thinking about asking Telma to leave with me. I thought I could do my best to give her and the boy a better, more up-standing life than the one she was living here.

"Hey, boy." A gravelly voice sounded, throwing off my train of thought. "You're the one at our gathering, a few weeks back, waiting the table, right?"

It was Henry's Uncle Matthew standing over me.

"Not sure I recall where you are referring to sir," I said.

"Hmmm. You even seem to have lost some of your nig-speak."

"I'z sorry, suh. I'm just doing my job here, playing this here contraption," I said, trying to get back the dialect.

"No, I'm sure you're the same one. Can you play something else besides Dixieland?"

"Yez, suh, I kin for sho,' what it be you's like ta hear?" I could hear my contrived tongue getting thicker and thicker with each word.

I prayed he would not ask for something I wasn't familiar with. I'd learned to play at least 30 songs by ear, enough to get by since learning Dixie.

"How about Beautiful Dreamer? Can you play that one, boy?"

"Yez suh, I kin."

I banged out the most powerful rendition of a song I'd only played twice in my entire life and hoped it would be enough to satisfy him.

I confirmed later that Henry's uncle was after me and that the dinner fiasco was not the only reason. Yes, the man connected me with the humiliation he suffered in my presence that terrible Sunday afternoon, but he was also investigating the young Negro I befriended on the train. Ezra it seems, was a wanted man for good reason—they believed he killed a white man back in North Carolina. He had run off and was a suspected accomplice in a train robbery just hours before he boarded the train with me in Memphis, and likely other armed train robberies across the South. The papers reported that he was just that cunning enough, along with another man, who was white, to avoid the law for over a year. They attributed a string of twenty robberies to the two bandits. If I knew of Ezra's poor character, or was privileged to the words Henry had whispered in his uncle's ear's at dinner that evening, I might have been prepared for the battle ahead. It wasn't until it was too late that Henry finally shared those words with me.

"I had to lean over and whisper into my uncle's ear what he needed to hear about himself." Henry added, "I was outraged at his conduct regarding Negroes as beasts."

I needed to know *exactly* what he said to set his uncle off after me.

"What did I say? Well, I'll tell you just what I told him. It's what he already knew, but will never accept. I said, 'I seem to remember mother telling father that you have at least a couple of offspring who are "half-beast" as you say.' Yes, and judging from the way he stormed out–which was not my intent–my uncle heard me loud and clear."

I knew Henry must've said something that cut his uncle in two, 'cause he left raising a storm, cursing hell-fire and damnation into the lives of everyone left behind in that dining room.

So it was Henry's uncle "thumping" outside of my window a few weeks ago, when Henry came over with the Ciaok look-alike. He must have been trying to get something on his nephew whom he probably despised now. I'm sure he heard me talking minus my dialect and went go to the sheriff with his suspicions.

If this thing with his uncle hadn't happened, I would have never known what Henry's profession was, or if he even had one. It wasn't a Negro's place to ask a White man who came into the saloon what he did for a living—no matter how friendly he was. I had assumed Henry worked at the bank or was one of those top men at the postal service who had to stay in other towns on business from time to time.

"But you can trust us." Henry said, in my room that day with his friend who—I found out—was also a lawyer. Henry said he worked with many others like him, but couldn't take a chance of making it widely known when they were in the Deep South.

When Henry told me he was a lawyer, and again, that he could help me, I didn't think there was anything he could do, even if it was his uncle after me. So when I ran into Henry, as I was hurrying out of the post office that morning, I walked right past him without saying a word.

CH 27

*(M)*olly

I'd come over to the Neuman's to check on Ma on her first day back on the job. As I stood around the back of the house listening, I could hear everything. I heard someone from my past whom I wanted to forget. A woman was paying Ma a visit. My endearing name for this woman had been 'cantankerous fang-fighter' and another one I remember was 'mean, moldy old crone'. I ran to the side where I could see and hear everything through an open window.

"Hello there, Miss Jean. Mrs. Neuman is not home right now," Ma said.

"Morning, Enola, I came to see you," the woman said, as she stepped inside the house.

"Why would you be wanting to talk to me, madam?" Ma asked, since this was Mrs. Neuman's cousin.

"You and I should be kind of like friends, Enola. I've been here a long time. I know I was away for a while, but I was here for a long time before then," Miss Jean said. "When you and your husband first met on the Neuman farm, and later when you had both Jake and Molly. I didn't go back up North for a while, not until Molly was about five, I believe. By then, your man was long gone."

Ma's eyes pressed shut, and she brought her hands up to her ears to close off to the sound of the women's voice.

"Did you hear me, Enola?" Miss Jean wanted to know.

Another moment passed. Ma closed the front door and stepped back, so I had to change my position at the side window.

"Yes, I heard you, Miss Jean," Ma said, seeming to get back her composure. "But it's so early for you to come knocking on the Neuman's door this morning."

Miss Jean waited, then began again.

"You know why I'm here, now?"

Ma paused.

"No, I don't."

"I see that Molly stayed in Boston longer than anyone expected, but now she's back. And where is Jake? I would have thought he would have sent for you and her by now." she said

I ducked down when Ma looked around the entry hall to see if anyone else was nearby.

"Look Miss Jean, if you here for trouble, I don't want none of it. I got enough and I am just able to get back to the Neumans to start back to doing my job now. So if you want to cause me harm, there ain't much more you can do that ain't already been done to me."

Jean gazed down at Ma's sturdy, worn shoes, then back up to her frayed apron, before looking into Ma's tired eyes. Miss Jean then made Ma an offer.

"Look, Enola, I just want to help. I know why Jake left. I think he knows what he shouldn't know, and that's why he hasn't sent for you or come back. I would like to help you get him back, if I can," she said.

Ma acted like she didn't know what Miss Jean meant. I thought the last person who would have any idea what happened to Jake would be Miss Jean Jackson.

Dressed in all yellow, like it was Easter Sunday, the woman didn't flinch, waiting for Ma to say something. She rang out in the only way I knew her to when someone thought they'd gotten the best of Ma and believed that they had trapped her in fear.

Ma recited her verse: "'Fear thou not, for I am with thee. Be not dismayed, for I am thy God.' Isaiah 41:10.'"

Standing face -to -face Miss Jean took a step back from Ma and shook her head. I knew Ma to find favor where there was none.

"Bejesus," Jean said. "If you're saying you believe in something higher than you, well, anyone can say that. But the truth still stands."

I almost applauded, when Ma stepped around to the door, opened it, then squared her shoulders and locked her steely eyes with her persecutor.

"You believe its right to aim to threaten a body for your own means," she said, "So when you got the chance and supposed you could get something—you followed it."

Then Ma took another step forward, now standing nose to nose with Miss Jean.

"Yes," Ma pronounced, picking up her worn bible from the side table, "you are right about one thing–the truth still stands."

I was shaking and hoped I didn't have to jump through the window and get in between them. The two women were glaring at each other with the outside door flung wide open. The wind blew leaves into the front hall, swirling in from the rambling, white-columned porch.

Ma put her bible down and broke the silence.

"Good day, ma'am."

It seemed 'miss insecure albatross'——my new name for Miss Jean—didn't want any more of a confrontation. She threw her head back and stomped past Ma, who slammed the door and locked it behind her.

I never let on that I was there that day.

CH 28

(*M*)

It had turned colder outside, but today was still wash day. I'd gathered up the months' laundry and set it next to the metal tub full of heated pump water and the washboard bonded inside a wooden frame. Ma went over to the kitchen shelf that held several bars of laundry soap. I started scrubbing the underthings first and moved on to the outer garments, resting the soap on the washboard between pauses from the strenuous up and down motion.

Ma reached for the hand wrung pieces to dip them into the rinse water, twist them again, and take out to hang on the clothesline to dry. The two lines had been there for as long as I could remember hooked from the back of the shanty to the outhouse in back. In between scrubbings she mentioned a chat we had the other day and related a conversation we had years before–which I'd forgotten. Now that it was just the two of us we seemed to be getting even closer–talking more.

She reminded me that I once asked a prickly question. That was years ago after I watched the preacher dancing on Sunday morning, down front at Blackjack Missionary Baptist. I was about seven, then.

"What does it mean to be happy?" I yelled, after hearing an elderly woman, sitting between us, whisper her thoughts about the minister to Ma. I must have been louder than necessary, 'cause she and the other ladies in the church that day turned, looked at me, and wagged their finger at me.

Considering our current situation, I guess Ma thought it was important to remind me of that question I'd asked so long ago, Ma also reminded me that when we'd left the church for home that day, she'd answered me.

"Joy is better," Ma said, "It's more enduring, and don't change 'cause of the things that happen to you in this world."

Ma held my little hand that afternoon so long ago, ending with, "You can choose joy, Molly 'cause it don't depend on people or what they do and that's all you need to survive to make your way."

Wringing out a blue blouse, I said, "I remember that talk now. But my mood has always been very susceptible to circumstances."

Ma laughed.

"I guess folks wonder how I can get along in life this way. But I try to make sure the circumstances go my way. If they don't, I lash out." I added.

Ma sighed and raised her eyebrows.

We walked back inside and sat for a while before I tried to defend myself.

"I am trying to change Ma, and doing well, but I wonder now, what's so wrong about my approach? Do you remember reading how colored participation in Virginia politics after the Civil War peaked last year when the Readjusters, the party of coloreds, swept statewide offices and took control of both houses of the assembly in Virginia?"

"Yes Molly, but you remember also reading about what they did to our beloved President Garfield, who didn't mince words by saying he was for equal rights for all Negros. I will always believe it was folks like some of these here who had something to do with his killing at that train station last July in Washington D.C. President Garfield had been our leader less than a year.

We became silent after that. I watched out the window at sunbeams bouncing off the clothes hung out to dry. Then I studied the new creases around Ma's eyes. She leaned back against the soft chair, listening to the mockingbirds on the roof as they chirped and sang. They were free from strain and obligation, and able to survive in their untroubled world.

Breathing softly, I closed and opened my eyes enough to notice the descending songbirds. They prompted me to get up and look out the back window at gray clouds moving in. Ma followed me outside to check if the clothes on the line were dry.

Before stepping out the back door, she spoke, saying something she must have been saving up for awhile.

"Did you know Mr. Neuman asked me to come live in the estate house? He said I could stay in that downstairs area in the back. You remember the one with the

185

L- shaped bedroom, double door closet, and sitting area with a bay window."

I coughed, not knowing how to respond, but Ma did it for me.

"I turned him down though, 'cause I don't need no one feeling bad for me. No need to speak of this again, Molly." She finished by stepping outside. I watched her pulling clothespins from canary yellow sheets whipping in the wind.

Battling hard to suppress my curiosity, there was no chance to say or ask Ma anything. I didn't always understand Ma, and I wondered how much better I did after she told me this. But I honored her wish and would not question her or her decision.

****

Certain setbacks here at home kept hurling me back to Boston. I would lie in my bed at night and think about being there. Sometimes the past and present of my life collided.

CH 29

(M)

I don't know about other folks, but I was never one to go in for kissing, especially on kin we visited within miles of these nearby parts of Grenada County and other places of the Mississippi Delta. Like on the Neuman estate and most other places in the south, in the last two years, several of our relatives and others had bought their own land outright and were not sharecropping.

Anyway, about kissing, something which my folks couldn't understand, and no one else, not even Aunt Minnie agreed with... For me, there was no darn way I would accept innocent pecking with anyone, especially my own cousin—even if I didn't know he was my cousin at the time.

Which leads me to John. Other than the obvious color thing, there were times, before I knew the whole truth, when I wondered why his mother, Mr. Neuman's sister kept trying to keep us apart. In their eyes there's me, from the hills of Grenada, living in a dilapidated shack, child of a sharecropper, and not fully aware of what to do or when to keep my mouth shut with society folks. Anyway, up North, they looked a little less terrified when I spoke out, but not by much. Still, their eyes grew as wide as those giant penny gumballs in ole' Mr. Richmond's mercantile.

Ah, Boston.

How I miss dear, outrageous Aunt Minnie, my love, after Ma and Alex (I guess). I remember the places she took me, The Smithsonian Institution in Washington, D.C. for one.

It snowed that day. Crystal flakes were falling from a milky gray sky. I dived into the white blanket covering, touching the freezing snow, felt its bumpy texture and fluffiness in my hands and against my face.

In her way, Aunt Minnie gave me as good of an education as I could have gotten anywhere. That same day she took me around and showed me the lovely row house she used to live in when she was in the South End before she moved to Back Bay, Boston. Would anyone believe those fashionable, single-family houses were built together, right next to each other, with absolutely no space in between? Three and four- stories tall, they looked almost just alike and sat on filled-in marshland.

Aunt Minnie said she'd only moved to Back Bay about five years ago. That means she'd been living in her new house for about three years before I met her.

"They turned it into a lodging house," Aunt Minnie said. "It makes it more affordable and easier for some of the newer residents to manage."

"So more than one family lives in there now?" I asked, marveling at how big it would be just for one family, but not as big as the Neuman place.

"Yes, I think they lent the rooms out to some of the workers from the countryside who moved here for jobs." She added.

"Was that why you moved away? It still looks very nice, though," I said.

"I don't know.

"I hate to think I would act that way. I think it was more that I was alone then, after my husband died, and it just wasn't where I wanted to live anymore," she confessed.

"Is this where Mr. Neuman's sister lives?" I asked, looking at two horse-drawn carriages slowly move past us on the cobblestone sidewalk.

"Yes, she still lives here, just a few blocks away. Since I invited her to the first 'affair' I gave in your honor last month, she has invited you over for a visit. We just have to find the time," Aunt Minnie said, stepping off the sidewalk to stride across the paved street. I hurried up close behind, just listening.

"I'm sure Walter never mentioned that his sister and her husband were one of the first immigrant families that settled in the South End during the early '60s. And I, for one, have no concerns with the Germans and Irish that have come to the U.S. They have brought some other religious congregations, built new churches, and opened quite a few stores on the first floor or downstairs ground levels of these buildings." She pointed out.

189

"Every man has to make a living, somehow," Aunt Minnie concluded.

****

That same sentiment ran through my head when Ma asked me to pick up some things for her, the next day, at the mercantile. Mr. Neuman allowed the strange Mr. Stratt to drive me to town, 'cause it was such a scorcher out that afternoon, which was very unusual for late April.

"You and yo' ma been all through that Neuman place, working and all." Stratt blurted after we rode for a while.

"Yes," I worked there a bit before I went to Boston," I said.

And I'm sure the entire town remembers what happened after I started working there too, I thought.

"I hear tell the place is the size of Californ-i-a on the inside," Mr. Stratt said.

"It's more than a mite's mass that's for sure," I said, knowing he was just fishing for gossip, which he wasn't going to get from me.

As we rode into town, I decided to bypass ole' Mr. Richmond's Mercantile and see what I could pick up at that Freedman's store. They set it up when I was eight and somehow survived until now. I hadn't been there for a few years and had since heard that Sarah, the girl Jake had tried to court, quit to get married.

Mr. Richmond stepped out front as we approached in Mr. Neuman's coach and drove past his store. "I reckon he be looking lil' green around the gills 'cause we're passing up his place." Mr. Stratt said, grinning.

"I can give someone else my business this time," I said, "other people have a family to feed and bills to pay too."

"Yas…suh…he sho' don't want you to do dat," he said. " Hear tell…he wonts to git dat Freedman place for his sister's boy… plans to git it for 2 bucks a month rent and lo and behold the man in there now paying the town 6 bucks for it."

Mr. Stratt seemed to be tickled about how much he knew concerning the town's inner workings.

"Yas suh…but this one here don't give a flying fricassee what you wonts." He said glancing at me, then back at Richmond's store.

"Hee…hee…he's seeing green alright…that's for sho'," Mr. Stratt laughed all the way to the Freedman's store.

CH 30

(*M*)

Riding back home, I took in the tall green pines lining our path and thought about Ma , even Jake, and our life here; especially what Mr. Stratt had said earlier. I wondered why I'd never considered our mistreatment in that way before.

We were coming onto bright open flatlands– littered with newly planted crops, pasture, and a grassy meadow filled with emerging wildflowers. By the time I got home, so many thoughts were rushing at me. I put my head down on the kitchen table when Ma walked in the room and noticed I was tired and distracted. "You can't be strained with worry," she said.

Ma placed the sandwich she prepared in front of me. "You've got to keep your troubles in their place."

"Yes, Ma, I'm trying."

"I know you are. I ain't gonna tell you all I've been through these last few years either, but I will tell you something..." she paused and then added, "A sharp mind and body go hand in hand. One holds up the other. Just like a doctor needs patients to keep his practice going; and people gone need doctoring from time to time. One's gone always need the other to keep going."

I picked up half of the fried catfish sandwich and took a small bite.

"That's how you live this here life to the fullest... I'll say it again," she said, putting her hands in her apron pockets, "You can't be strained with worry... your thoughts going everywhere. Keep your troubles in their place, pay them no mind when they try to get your attention—cause if you don't, for sure, they'll take over."

But worry was all I could do. I thought about one of the last talks Jake and I had when I was with him at the lake.

"Jake, you are always so giving to everyone, especially Ma. Don't you ever want to tell other folks where to put their ornery ways?"

"They won't take nothing like that from me. Now you, on the other hand..." Jake had said laughing, but then he saw that I was being serious, so he stopped laughing and got serious too.

"Okay, I see you don't get it. They won't take from me what they will accept from you, Molly. Don't you get it?" he said.

"No, I don't. I just get that you are making excuses for not standing up for yourself."

193

After I said that, Jake's voice rose and his eyes stretched wide.

"You don't know how many times I wished I could be like you. Say what I feel and not care about what happens after that!"

I took a step back to take a good look at this "other" brother–his eyes fierce, dark and fiery. I felt something twist in my stomach when I caught that look from him.

"You've sounded off so many times to so many people," Jake said. "And nothing horrible... thank God... has happened to you."

He swallowed and kept going. "But maybe there are some scars cut deep into Ma and me. Maybe we saw something so terrible happen to someone close to us that all 'your so-called gumption' was knocked right out of us."

My legs trembled then, while I looked for something to hold on to...a tree, a branch, anything. I grabbed hold of a jagged limb and then clapped my eyes onto the leaves that were rustling across in front of me.

"Look at me, Molly," Jake commanded. "You hear what I say?"

I had stiffened at the hoarse crack in his voice.

"You don't remember anything about Pa, do you?" Jake said. Creases lined his forehead.

I shook my head.

"Every Sunday, he got up like a jackal. Nobody could say anything to wipe that sneering frown off of his face. His squinting eyes would dart from Ma to me, then to you sitting on Ma's lap or lying in your box."

My usual calm brother, now had beads of sweat on his forehead and his eyes looked steely and determined.

I didn't know what to say. Jake had never said anything like that about Pa. He always said he was little more than in knee britches when Pa left. Jake hardly ever said anything about Pa. When he did, nothing was ever bad. I guess he lied.

Suddenly Jake broke off, "I don't know why I said that."

I remember Jake searching out the brown wooden outside-stool we kept hidden in the hollowed-out big oak. He plopped down on it, his head hung low. Then he leaned from one side to other, going back and forth, as if he was trying to rock something loose.

"I reckon I wasn't that old anyhow, maybe six or seven," he said, "So what did I know 'bout folk's ways, leastwise a man's life?"

I leaned forward, trying to catch his gaze, hoping to communicate that he struck me as confused—falling back into his old way of talking—not proper at all.

"Maybe you should ask Ma about it," I said.

"Naw, past is past, and we were talking about our lives now. My life and why I act different from you."

I nodded.

"So now–this day, do you think I am worth so much to anyone else–besides you and Ma–that they wouldn't think twice about lynching me if I acted anything like you?"

I'd opened my mouth to say something, closed it, and then opened it again, stuttering.

"B-but God…a-a-and Mr. Neuman…a"

Jake broke in with a sneer.

"There you go again with Mr. Neuman. At least you mentioned God first before you thought of him."

When I let go of the bumpy branch that I'd latched onto, a few leaves tumbled to the ground. Jake's criticism had me pacing around the familiar willow-oak tree in search of an answer.

"Why would you believe I'd put Mr. Neuman above God? I know he's been good to us and I don't agree with everything Ma says about God, but it's still her house and she believes God sees what's happening to us here in this world and will help us—even someone like you," I chided.

This was as good a time as any to goad my older brother. Other girls around here loved to point out, though I never noticed, how Jake's smile always stretched across his sculptured face.

"Aaah-ha, my itsy, bitsy little sister. Do you honestly believe my time here on earth, means that much to Him?" Jake asked, pointing upwards.

After that, we just dawdled, without saying a word to each other. I breathed in the clean, early evening air. It was getting dark before either of us spoke again. By then Jake was lying on the ground, looking dazed, staring overhead. I'd gotten up to check if any pecans were ready enough to take back. The trees at Milcreek Pond usually ripened sooner than the pecan tree by our house. Near darkness always brought me thoughts of what some used to say about my favorite place. How people used to believe something spooked the woods with 'lost souls' crying out in the night, floating in the thick forest brush. It was said folks would steer clear of the deep wooded part of Milcreek Pond, back then. I put that out of my mind, particularly the time Jake said Ma mentioned some unspeakable things happened not long ago in those woods. Things too terrible to talk about.

I jumped when Jake blurted out something. It brought my thoughts back from the shadows.

"Indigo Sky."

"What? It's time we should get going....who's she, anyway? I'd said.

Jake laughed.

"It's not a girl, you little biddy."

"Something you wrote, I bet?" I said.

"Yeah, I guess."

"Look up there, "he said, "At the way the world looks as we approach the night."

"You're saying that's an actual name of the color of the sky? I just thought it was a plant they used to grow."

I decided to make something humorous out of what he was so obviously trying to point out to me, since he wanted to call me a "biddy," like I were an old maid or something. Anyway, it felt good to get him away from being too serious and that strange talk about Pa.

"O-o-r-r is it really the name of that girl, uh-huh," I said, "The one you liked in Mr. Temple's class."

I watched for his reaction, hoping to see him blush and hide that bashful grin. He didn't.

"It is about the sky, but more. And no, I said it's not a girl's name."

"So is it about a boy named Sky?" I goaded.

"No dummy, not a person at all. And it's not just about sky color, either, not to me."

"Well, what is it?" I said.

"When I look up, I see the deep expanse of our lives," Jake explained. "Yours, mine, Ma's, even Pa's– who   I hardly remember and you don't even know– and everyone else's, too."

I wanted to ask, *"If you don't even hardly know him, then how can you remember Pa being ornery, like you said earlier?"*

But I didn't. I just went back to listening. Jake wasn't done talking.

"Everything is so rich, deep, endless," Jake added. "Still bright somewhere, above what we can see and I want to find that reflective light that gives everything its beauty and wonder."

Jake stretched out his long legs, then closed his eyes for a moment.

I couldn't stop myself this time.

Thinking about Pa again, huh? I said.

"Were you even listening to me?" Jake asked. "You weren't. Why do I waste my time?"

"No, I heard about the sky and all too, but I think you were thinking about Pa when you were looking up at your indigo sky; more than about Ma and me, that's all."

Jake nodded.

"I do remember once talking to Him," he pointed above, "You know, like we see Ma do every day. I asked Him why some folks lives are worth so much more than others?"

At first I thought he was back to talking about Pa, but Jake said no. Then, I was about to poke my big brother for not listening to me and ignoring my question about Pa, but he didn't look in the mood. So, I kept following whatever direction he wanted to take this conversation.

"Well, did He answer?" I asked.

"I don't know, but I did get the notion after asking Him… that none of our lives here matter so much," he said.

"How'd you get that, if you don't know if He answered?"

"I dunno. " Jake let out a long sigh, and just looked at me.

I guess we both thought that this conversation was going nowhere.

But then Jake brought up something else.

"When I look around, Molly, the only thing I see is those who have the most. They manage to convince each other, and us ones who have little that their lives are worth more to Him than ours."

"What do you mean?" I asked.

"Oh…I dunno…. I'm here, having to live in this here body," Jake said, "I have to manage with this portion I'm given. It don't matter what I believe."

I waited while he thought of something else to say.

"But, I did write about it once," Jake said.

"Some of your writings, huh?"

I thought about what that kind of thinking, like those thoughts he just brought up, would look like on paper—especially coming from him.   "So you think we're all just worth the same to Him–or nothing at all?" I said.

I didn't really believe that, but I had hoped the finality of my statement would stop Jake from acting different than I was used to. He said nothing, so I went on to say what I really thought.

"Well, I hope you don't go showing something you wrote about that–to Ma," I said. "So don't say anything to her about your kind of thinking. Especially not you."

"Never said I would say something to Ma, just telling you that's all," Jake said, "You asked."

I thought, I don't recall asking anything. When we got home that night, I snuck into his room, while he was outside, and got a look at a sheet of writing he'd left on his table– to see what I was up against. I didn't need him to get into trouble with Ma —turning into me. The page was written in his special script. I think he would be wise to stay the way he is and keep his writings out of his actions.

Reflections in the ocean…like that above
You, me, family, everyone enclosed
The skies are always there above us,
Look away if you dare.
But… it will go on long after you,
Forever a sea of blue.
I'm same as you
Look at me
I'm part of the tapestry
Just a darker hue
Call me Indigo
Still seeing, believing
It's night now
Deeper, yet still bright
Forever, and ever and ever blue

CH 31

(M)

Our home was not really all that run down. It was a well-built place that looked a lot better inside after Ma and I spent the past few months cleaning and dusting regularly. The other day, it took the both of us to move the stove and heavy table in the kitchen. The long, brown, tweed couch in the living room was no easy task either. We finally shifted it, pushing and pulling, inch by inch away from the wall on that side, far over enough to sweep and mop the floor underneath.

Cleaning, pushing, stooping, and bending for over five hours, drove me to get washed up afterwards, getting water from the outside pump. After Ma was done using it, we added lye soap, and then placed the morning dishes in for a good scrubbing.

When we'd first started with the cleaning last month, Ma has started looking miserable again, but now her face was missing the lines and her eyes were getting brighter.

She was even smiling more. Maybe it would help her to accept things even more if she knew about the burlap bag hiding under Jake's bed.

I wanted to show her his writings, but I had to get her ready first.

"Ma you know all three of us, you, me and Jake, we were all so different, you know, in the way we thought and did things," I began preparing her.

"Molly…your brother is always the one who's been more like me," she said, putting her hand to her chest. "Now you say he isn't really like me much? Maybe it's a good thing. Look at what being my way has got me. Your Pa gone and now Jake staying away from me this long."

Oh…no…please don't get sick again…I thought. You thinking Jake's still alive—and now bringing up Pa. You never brought him up. I took this as a sign that maybe I should bring him into this, too. It couldn't hurt. Maybe it would get her to finally accept reality.

"Ma look at it this way, if Pa is gone and now this year Jake is gone—the way you see it—isn't it sort of an honor to go early… even better than a dream, when you get more time with the man upstairs?"

Ma's mouth stretched into a straight line across her face, while her eyes flashed open and close. She jumped up so fast her chair fell back, causing her apron string to get caught on the table, pull loose and fall to the floor, almost tripping her as she stormed out of the room.

I ran behind her, scared now, and tapped on the closed door. "Ma, what did I say wrong?"

She swung open the bedroom door, clutched the frame, and shrieked at me waving her other arm in the air. "You...you and your dreams. We don't even know what's going to happen from one moment to the next or one day to the next, much less one year to the next. I don't want to hear any more about dreams, going early, or anything else to do with being gone again. DO YOU HEAR?"

I didn't understand, since that other world was what *she* used to talk about. I dragged my feet past her into the next room to sit by the window and wish for better days. I let her calm down and crept away to console my hurt feelings by returning to the place I should have never left.

****

It was a bright sunny Sunday when Aunt Minnie took me to meet her friend, Dr. Elizabeth Blackwell, from Bristol, England, she'd opened a hospital for women and children in New York. She welcomed anyone who couldn't afford the doctors who demanded fees many poor souls couldn't pay. Some barely had enough to eat. Aunt Minnie said the lady only became a doctor because a dying friend of hers was treated as less than a person by the man who was her doctor. Dr. Elizabeth believed that if her friend had had a woman doctor, she would have gotten the compassion she wanted so much while she was wasting away.

"You are a lot like Dr. Elizabeth, Aunt Minnie," I said, after we'd left her office.

"How's that 'pretty one'?" asked Aunt Minnie, using the nickname she'd given me.

"You never take on people about anything they say or do to you," I said, "it's usually about how they are treating someone else. You don't have to even know the person or care about them to stand up for them."

"That's the way I was made. From a little girl, I've been this way. Don't know why I didn't let other's notions of what was morally right and wrong sway me. I had my own ideas."

"Maybe you're an angel or a saint or something," I said staring above, "Saint Millicent."

"Stop that, girl. That's something I'm surely not. You've got me blushing. You are something. You know that?"

We giggled like the girlfriends we were. As snow began to fall, we headed towards the city park where a group of children were already skating. I'd practiced throughout the previous winter and had gotten good at it. I had on my slightly shortened skirt that day to reduce the risk of my tripping and falling on the ice. Since everyone now considered ice skating a healthy form of exercise, much like dancing and appropriate for ladies, we could enjoy ourselves. I couldn't wait.

****

Ma tiptoed into the doorway, the sight of her reined my thoughts back in. I followed her back out to find she had tried to finish the cleaning and cooking, doing everything herself, as if I wasn't there.

Taking a dish out of her hand, I said, "Ma, I came back home to help you and that's what I'm going to do."

It was my choice to make, and I did.

"Ma, I know that you know better than anybody else that times are hard, but they are getting better, aren't they?" I hoped that they were.

She nodded, picking up the checkered cleaning rag from the side of the tub.

"You know, we make our own choices," I added, speaking my mind carefully now. "Most of what happens to us is due to purposeful decisions we've made. Then we have the gumption to get mad with other folks when they get good results from their choosing, and we don't."

I felt myself going off on a tangent about something, but I didn't know how to turn back.

"If we ordain someone else's life as better, then we chalk it up to fate or something for them. Or say, God likes them better."

Ma stopped washing, put the dish away, and sat down.

"So, are you saying that I have free will and am responsible for the choices I make in my life, just like that person I may spend all my time ranting about—thinking they have it better?" She said.

I moaned–setting down a dried glass breakfast dish. I didn't want Ma to think I meant her.

"Oh, no. I don't mean you or the things in your life you can't control, Ma," I said, picking up the same glass dish, I tried to think of some other way to explain what I meant.

"Okay…it's like Jake's decision to leave, verses my getting sick when I was little and having a slight limp, even now–at times. Things like that… no need to fret about *one* of the two—my getting sick was out of my control. But what does one do when they can make a choice to do or not to do something—while they're still young and have their health like Jake— and they make the wrong decision? Then someone else makes and things turn out right for them."

"I know you didn't mean me…" Ma said, ignoring my last example and going back to what I said before, "I was just using myself to understand your thinking. It's all so hard—whether you have a choice or not. It's true, Jake could have controlled whether he left or not even with all those stumbling blocks he felt pushed him away."

Maybe I was guilty too, at first, of being envious. I thought–polishing the same glass dish for a third time.

"I guess it's like when I first made up my mind not to stay up North even longer, after you didn't come to visit last spring. I told Aunt Minnie that I had to come back, 'cause you'd stopped writing and I missed you. On the trip back, I got jealous thinking about Jake and how he got to stay up North– making his way."

Not knowing he never made it.

"And we don't know for sure that he didn't get North," Ma said, as if reading my thoughts.

I kept talking, walking over to put the dish away now, stalling long enough to figure out a way to respond to her allusion that Jake was still alive. "I sometimes hate myself for being envious the way I was, but it's the truth. I felt that way towards Jake, and I was wrong, Ma"

I hope he did make it North.

CH32

(M)

The next morning I went out for an early walk to get some fresh air. I had to pass the Neuman place to get to the other side of Milcreek Pond, where I was headed. I was so wrapped up in trying to relax, I even draped the side of my face with a sheer covering. The way I was feeling and looking, I didn't want to see any- one. I was hoping to get down the dirt road unnoticed and find relief in the shady groves of welcoming pine, pecan, and towering willow-oak trees surrounding my "perfect oasis" at the other end of the Neuman estate.

Walking briskly, as I passed in back of the rambling white columned house, I held my breath and froze when I saw Mrs. Neuman with one of her 'garden party' friends strolling my way from across her elaborate garden filled with rows of irises, violets and asters. Tussling with this woman at the restaurant was more than enough for me.   Now that I knew the reason she treated me so fierce was no fault of mine, I had decided not to even acknowledge her. I'd reformed from those days where I could only hold my tongue for so long. Anyway, I had enough to handle with Jake being gone and Ma the way she was. I had planned to just walk past her, maybe nod, nothing more. I promised myself not to say anything to her, good or bad.

I kept my word best as I could... what happened next was not my fault.

With my nose in the air, ears shut off, and head turned away, I could still detect it wasn't her 'garden party' guest–woman in the eatery the other night–who spoke first.

"You know you were right at the restaurant...they didn't teach her anything about how to be a lady up there in Boston. Just think, I'm from nearby, in Maine, and I even remember that it is of the utmost decorum that you pay a greeting to a lady when you walk past her home."

"I so agree." The other voice said.
Still looking in the opposite direction and nearly past the garden, I gritted my teeth together–holding my tongue captive until it hurt.

"And have you heard anything from your long-lost brother, dear?" she sniped loudly, "See, little girl, that's how a lady acts. She asks about your relations."

My neck swung around until it popped into place in her direction.

"Oh, I know how to recognize a lady," I said, "When one finally presents herself."

My eyes were wide and head on a swivel going from one woman to the other, and all around the garden, looking for the missing 'lady'.

"Until that time," I added, "I treat scum like the dirt it is."

There was no going back now, Ma wasn't here to help me stop.

"My...my, what big fangs we have." Mrs. Neuman crowed.

"Not fangs, just reinforcement," I said, "It only comes out at night."

"It's daylight, you little idiot," her sidekick quipped.

"In a place like this, with folks like you," I said, "It's always dark as night."

I strutted off in the direction I was planning to go, determined to do everything I could to forge a different route back home; even if it meant traveling to the other side of the tree-lined pond to avoid ever again being ambushed along the way.

****

CH 33

(J)ake

I felt something akin to ice brushing against my arm. Lying close to the window, I knew the cover was off, since I didn't figure it was cold out. I grabbed the heavier covers, pulled them up around my neck, and finally flung them to the floor. If I get too warm and relaxed I'd have the same vision, just like the one I had last week and the week before. But this one wasn't really a delusion, not like the other. In this dream, I got away before it became a nightmare, or a glimpse of what my life would have been if I stayed.

I wiped the crust away from the inner corners of my eyes, and mumbled quietly, reliving the images still in my head and words hidden away on paper.

Again she showed up, this time up at the mill. "Look, I've asked you over and over again to leave me alone," I begged her.

"Ha, you don't have a choice, and you don't want more trouble," she said.

"Why don't you let me be?" I asked her.

She placed her index finger up to my open mouth and pressed her lips together.

"Shhh," she'd whispered, before putting slim, white gloves on her tiny, manicured hands. She patted her hair and waltzed out.

Against my brow, now dripping wet, I held the same white handkerchief I had that day. I got up and stumbled over to the wobbly chair in front of the wooden desk. I picked up my new fountain pen and writing tablet. I can't wait until I'm further north to contact Ma and Molly again, since Ciaok said they didn't get the first letter I mailed when I got to Memphis. But then they know that I'm okay by now, since they would have gotten the last two posts I'd sent back by Ciaok.

I put the pen down and crawled back into bed, hoping to get some rest before going to work today and wondering if I would ever be able to go back home while *she* was still there.

CH 34

Lena Neuman

Lena had played the attentive, devoted mistress of the Neuman estate for more years than she'd care to remember. After all those years, her hair was still the color of molasses, touched by minimal graying, her silky alabaster neck still glistened with sweet perfumed powder. She thought it was about time someone thought about how much she'd contributed to the success of her family, to the business, and everything that is impressive to others about the Neumans.

Her flashing, green eyes stared back at her in the looking glass. Who has the east coast roots? She thought to herself.

She wasn't some immigrant who had just come over on the boat in the past 40 years. Her people had been in that country since the early settlers landed on Plymouth

Rock. But she had taken it upon herself to fall for mister-up-and-coming German import. She was young and thought differently about everything. She was going to be the perfect wife and mother, despite her laughable attitude toward the constraints of finishing school and the act of blossoming into the perfect debutante. They were both bored into her soul by her socially conscious parents.

Lena thought, did her husband Walter think the two children they had together would wait until he and she were dead to get their share? What did he take them for? They'd fight him tooth and nail on that one. They'll come back South if only to sell what they get from both parents. If he was going to be this way with her, she thought– because she didn't treat his "little prize" like the princess she thought she was– then Lena believed she may just have to tell him once and for all what she knew.

Lena knew he didn't want such talk coming out into the open, because a scandal would tarnish his precious good name. But it didn't matter to Lena that no one else in Grenada had her husband's squeaky clean reputation. They considered him god-like around there and something like this would bring him down and hurt his business– she was sure of it.

Lena looked for her copy of the papers for days before realizing that Jake probably took it when he left. It was too hard to get another copy made from the original she had spied again this morning in her husband's office.

What had Jake planned to do with the documents? Lena had looked everywhere for them and was sure he had taken them. She had not been certain some ruthless hillbilly hadn't killed Jake before the trio she sent could find and question him about the deed. Those men she hired were just as dangerous and mad, especially since they didn't get their money after all the tracking they did. But she wasn't going to pay them for a job they hadn't done.

And Enola was of no use to her anymore. Lena had tried to ask questions about what was on the dead body that the sheriff showed her in Hardeman County.

Lately, the only consolation for Lena Neuman were days like today. She could begin the weekend talking to the one family member that she felt she could trust– her cousin visiting from Maine.

"That Molly's been back for over two months, and already I wish I hadn't seen her. Both times she's been nothing but trouble." Lena said, "I went on with my life after that terrible fire almost two years ago and am not going back to that little headache. It took so much time getting my house back in order. The second floor had to be completely redone, and the entire place had to be aired out. I can still smell the smoke from time to time." Lena ranted, as her cousin always let her do.

Lena's cousin, Harlan reached out to take her hand in one of his and gently patted the red-knuckled balled up fist with his other.

"I don't care what anyone says," Lena declared, without being asked, "I have moved on. Didn't I forgive our cousin Jean for the shenanigans she pulled, which ended up setting my house on fire? She belongs somewhere for patients. I do believe that's where she was years ago. Did you see her when she went back North for almost ten years? Only to resurface here now, an even older old-maid, causing another thorn in my side."

"You poor girl. You've been through a lot," he said. She rolled her eyes, sighing with gratitude for his understanding. "It's no wonder our uncle, Jean's father—that miserable old drunken cuss—died only six months after the fire. I'm sure the shame of it all killed him."

"Lena, I know how you must feel. And I also know Jean has been back for way more than two months, so it's not her you hated to see," he said.

Lena's lips parted, showing small white teeth.

"I don't know what I would do, if you didn't come down to visit a few times a year. I would be out of my mind."

"I wouldn't want the life you've had to live. You are a saint, my dear, a martyr."

Harlan put down the porcelain cup, reached across the table, and gently stroked the back of her open hand.

"How is dear, Cousin Jason?" She asked. "If only his previous visit, during the last Autumn Festival, wasn't cut short by the fire. I miss his visits now that he's married and moved all the way to that godforsaken Canada."

"I know. Now *we* have a bond that can't be broken," Harlan added.

"Let's not go there," she said.

"If you wish, my dear."

Lena knew it was time to change the subject and get back in a positive frame of mind by mentioning the upcoming trip to Spain, France and Italy.

"The next trip will be my busiest excursion, yet," she said.

"Let's stop in town tomorrow and get something for your travels. If you plan to visit all around Europe next spring, you've got to get started now. I still can't understand why you don't want me to come along. We would have a splendid time together in France, especially at La Tour Eiffel and then venturing south to the Rivera, Nice and Antibes," Harlan said.

"You know, the more I think about it, I may not make the trip," she said, patting her coiffured head.

"You're making fun of me now. What do you take me for?" he said.

"I mean it."

"You do?"

"Yes I do. I should stay home and encourage democracy from afar– show that we are the model state– lead by example," Lena said.

"Sno-o-ort. "

Lena hated Harlan's "nose laugh" where he blew air forcefully through his nostrils while he chuckled slightly...with his lips puckered.

"Okay, I'm lying," she said, "but if you can't pay your own way, Harlan, then Walter surely will not."

Silence hung like a canopy between the two of them.

"Well, do you plan to?" she asked.

"What do you think? This trip is for you. I'll be your much needed companion and guide. Don't tell me you don't want me with you?"

"What does what I want have to do with anything? And what would I need with a guide? I've been to Europe before. Remember that six-month grand tour I took back in 1860."

"But that was so long ago. You were just a young girl and didn't understand the ways of the world," he said with a smirk.

"Walter would shut down that precious mill of his and see his loyal workers hungry, before he'd pay for a second companion for my trip, least of all you!" she said.

"You know you have your ways of getting that big buck of yours to do what you want. Speaking of, have you caught up with the-gorgeous-Jake yet?"

"Shut up! Where do you get such language, cousin, and what happened to your gentlemanly stance?" Lena asked.

"Don't tell me to shut up. You shut up," he said.

"Let's stop this, Harlan. You're so trite. You're becoming quite earthy, like the empty-headed classless lot around here."

"Don't you dare compare me to these red-neck hicks." he said.

"Oh, they're not so bad. I tolerate this frontier country, since one of the few good things about them is they try to give themselves airs and class they don't have."

"All they have to do is open their mouths," he said, "and the suspense is over."

The pair laughed so hard that Harlan knocked the cup of tea over onto the oriental carpet. He then rang for the girl to come clean it up.

"Okay, okay, let's get back to business, I just think you don't want me to accompany you to Europe, that's all, and I'd like to know why?" he demanded.

Lena focused her attention on the untouched cucumber sandwiches centered on the porcelain plate.

Harlan set down his fresh cup and saucer and stared directly at her without blinking. His gaze forced Lena to look up.

"You know exactly what I'm thinking," he said.

Lena shot up. Her lovely cucumber sandwiches and dishes crashed to the floor.

"You go too, too far," she shouted.

Harlan's thin upper lip curled on its right side as he rose from the davenport and crossed to the opposite side of the parlor room. He parted the lime silk draperies which covered the white pane-glass window and looked out.

Lena headed toward the parlor doors and then stopped– waiting for an apology.

Harlan kept staring out the window until Lena finally huffed out, swinging both doors back to the wall.

"Bye-Bye, dear Lena," he chuckled.

****

"If my husband thinks I don't know, he's got another thing coming. I've known for years." Lena said aloud to herself, throwing down her hairbrush. "He couldn't hide something like that from a woman who has studied him from the first time she saw him, more than 20 years ago."

Lena noted the way he looked at Molly. If one didn't know better, you would think she was his woman. But Lena knew the truth.

The entrance doors in the front hall opened and closed loud enough to be heard upstairs.

He's home early, she thought.

"Lena."

It wasn't him at all, but her tiresome cousin Jean. She was back for a few months to visit. Two years ago, she was almost run out of town when everyone learned she started the fire that ruined Lena's celebrated Autumn Festival. Lena and Walter hadn't planned another gala, since. Lena believed fate was testing her, having Jean show up, just after she'd promised Harlan she'd forgiven the woman. Meeting her downstairs, Jean pulled Lena's face against her lips for their usual greeting.

"Dear, dear cousin Lena, it's been so long. It seems like years."

Lena noticed she spoke as if she should have forgiven her, by now, for almost burning her house to the ground.

"Jean," she said," I would offer you a cup of tea, but I'm positive you have to get going."

"No, I'll have some."

"As I said, you have to get going!"

The slightly older beleaguered-looking woman stood with her eyes wide and hands held out, as if asking what next?

"Lena, aren't you ever going to get over it? It was an accident? What can I do to make it up to you?"

Lena looked down at her cousin's sturdy foot covering waiting for her to make another offer.

"I see you are still trying to hide that hammertoe of yours," she said.

"Oh, stop Lena. "I've already done what you asked. I truly have. Just please, let's be friends again," Jean said.

"Did you find out if she knows anything?"

"She doesn't seem to know where he is, plus I think she's crazy."

"She's just putting on. We shall see. Here, use this if you have to."

"Lena, this is a gun."

"I know what it is. It's small enough to fit in your bag, if not, carry it in this. These goons around here will think you are hunting ducks or something." Lena said.

"Lena, I can't!"

"Look, it was you who almost burned my house to the ground, not even a few years ago, 'cause you couldn't get over I got Walter, and you didn't–. Now I think that boy went north looking for a lawyer to process those papers for his family. He'd never get them to do it for him here in Mississippi. No one has come here yet, and if Jake isn't dead, and if he's hiding somewhere with those papers, I've got to find him."

"But… Lena," her cousin pleaded.

"No! Get out of here, and do what I tell you!"

****

Exactly an hour after Jean left, Walter showed up, and Lena was back to her usual self.

"Hello-o-o dear, I didn't know it was so late," she called down.

Walter Neuman, whom Lena referred to privately as her "lover-of-mankind" husband, walked through the front double doors, looking older and wearier than his 45 years. Despite his rejuvenated interest in her the past two years, Walter had turned in–what she believed was– a pitiful performance as a husband these recent months.

"I'm early, I know. I have to visit a business in Duck Hill early tomorrow morning and I left some papers in my room I need to go through first. " Walter said.

Lena knew exactly what papers he was looking for. She'd seen them over two years ago and had them copied by hand. In Walter's bedroom office that morning, she saw the original copy and rifled through the pages a few minutes after he'd left. Again, he had left his connecting bedroom door unlocked, so she slipped through, as she did every morning. This time; however, Lena found something of interest spread across the settee in his sitting area. What caught her interest were the familiar descriptions scribbled across the pages. She didn't understand them when she first read the papers years ago. This time, Lena gathered them up and took them down to the parlor to show Harlan when he came over. She'd accidently left them there when she marched out in a fit of temper over his comments.

"But, I thought your machine supplier was in the other direction in Graysport? Do you need to look at papers right now?" she asked sweetly.

Walter kept moving. He headed through the entry hall, around the corner, and up the stairs to where he remembered leaving the papers that morning.

"No reason I shouldn't," Walter said.

Lena rambled on.

"Why don't you go into the dining room and I'll find the new girl, she's somewhere around here, and have her bring you a cup of tea first, or better yet, a good shot of whiskey to relax you."

"No Lena, I'm fine, I don't need a drink."

Lena knew this diversion would give her time to get near the parlor and grab the papers. With the documents in hand, Lena would try to dash back upstairs to Walter's sitting room, hoping to get there before he did. She'd spread the papers across the settee where he'd left them.

Walter had stopped. Then moved back down a stair. Turning, he called up to her.

"By the way, who is this new girl, you hired yesterday? Where is she from?"

Thank goodness, she thought. He's giving me some time.

"Oh---the new girl...well... her name... let me see...her name... uh, I didn't really think it was so important to remember her full given name when I hired her." Lena said, "I know the first name is Sally, but you're right, we should know both her first, middle and last names."

"Well, just the first and last is fine enough, and I don't have to know it right now. Just tell me about her, that's all," he said.

Lena continued talking, looking at him again, as he moved up the staircase.

"Oh, but you should also know her middle, dear. You should very well know the full names of anyone who is employed in this household. What if something happens to them or to us?"

She continued, "Oh yes, I agree 100 percent. You should know everything about her, including her middle name."

"Okay, Lena, either way, whatever you say," he sighed.

Walter's progress up the staircase had slowed. Lena was grateful that he was extremely tired from a long day.

She continued to rattle on.

"I'm just going to get that paper from the parlor where I left it. It's the one I wrote all the information down about the new girl. Just you wait right there, dear." She pointed at the stair on which he was standing.

"It will only take me a second now and with my notes we can discuss this young woman, I've brought into this house," Lena said.

He let out a long sigh.

"I'm not fine, *now*. I need a drink."

She reminded him. "After the list!"

Lena told herself, *I'm not going to be caught, not yet. I've been at this too long.*

She tucked her arm into his and pulled her husband's reluctant frame around and back down the winding staircase towards the dining room and left him there, a good distance from the parlor, where she was headed next.

"What are you doing, Lena?" he asked.

"Oh. I moved the liquor table into the dining area this morning. Just stay put and I will hand you your drink."

She ran out and into the parlor, quickly shutting the doors behind her. She was grateful Harlan, who had become completely exasperating, was long gone. He had left the papers on the table behind the davenport.

She gathered them together and turned each page over so the blank side would show on top—the way Walter left it. There was a fountain pen and torn slip of paper sitting next to the pile, so she jotted down that Sally girl's last name, which she'd known all along.

After leaving the dining room, Walter made his way back to the stairs. Now on the landing, he headed upstairs towards his closed bedroom door.

"Got to get in that room before him," Lena mumbled to herself.

"Dear, dear, now why didn't you wait?" she called out.

Lena's voice climbed an octave higher as she ran up the stairs ahead of him.

"Here, here now. Let me take those things and put them away for y—o-u," Lena insisted. She proceeded to grab at Walter's jacket with him still in it, and then at his leather boots.

"Lena, what are you doing now?"

"Walter, you just waltz up these stairs without taking your things off." She shook her finger at him. "Now we'll have none of this. Let me have your jacket. And your hat."

Crossing his bedroom floor, Lena kept talking loud enough for her husband to hear behind her.

"That's why I'll be so pleased when that Sally girl starts. Then you won't have to lug all your things up the stairs to your room."

Lena wasn't even sure what she was saying, but she didn't care, as long as it worked.

She made it across the room, keeping ten paces in front of her husband. Once Lena stepped into his sitting area, she placed the documents back, just as she had found them. She was grateful the area wasn't visible from the doorway–where he was still standing– and was hidden by two well-placed ornamental pillars.

Lena pulled the pages from behind her back and slipped them underneath her husband's jacket. She then placed them onto the settee below the window, without making any detour steps.

"Lena, the drink?" he asked.

"Oh, yes, that's right. You do need one, I insist."

All that evening and for the next few days, those papers and an incident had cropped back up into Lena's mind. Once she believed she'd learned the reason Walter was so distracted and nervous.

Now that her husband's other daughter had come back, Lena made up her mind to take care of that problem for good. Seeing those papers again, Walter left in his sitting area, confirmed even more than she'd thought she remembered about their finances and how much the Neumans were worth.

She lamented that she had left her handwritten copy of those papers for just a few hours in that safe at the mill… just that one day. And Jake had access to the safe before he left.

"Jacob McCray… Enola's precious little Jake," Lena said aloud to herself. "But I know him better than anyone and would have welcomed him back if he'd just given up those papers. Afterwards, I would have made it such a satisfactory experience for him all around and so worth his while. But there's no chance of that now."

She sat down at her dressing table, took out four long hairpins and loosened her hair, letting it fall to her shoulders for the night.

CH 35

(J)ake

I got up the next morning and struggled to get ready for the day ahead. I didn't sleep well last night. But, at least I didn't have that one particular strange dream again. This time, it was one I'd had before– but not since I'd been posing as Jeremiah. In the dream, instead of Ma talking to Molly about me and me listening about what had happened, I am now a part of the scene. I was the character, a participant in the action I envisioned last night.

In it, I see a man dressed like a preacher, and he is praying over me, just like Ma said. I told him, with a firm nod and set jaw, I was already saved. But the preacher wouldn't stop praying and casting out some- thing the preacher said he could see in me. My eyes seemed to shut tight for a moment, and when I opened them, there were three people where the preacher once stood. I'd never seen these people before.

I got up through a door and down a flight of stairs away from them. Then stumbled at the bottom and looked up at a transom over the door. The three faces at the top looked down at me from over the opened transom.

"Do you know these people," a voice said. It was a question from the preacher, as he stood behind me. "Someone must have left the door open," the man added.

Then Pa appeared, standing there in place of the preacher, and he went to get his rifle 'cause we didn't know those people who were now banging on the door at the top of the stairs. One of them, after I took a harder look, appeared to have the countenance of a woman. That person backed down and circled back around to a lower door in the cellar and I knew she would come back up if she could find her way through the unlocked door.

I stood up and rushed to the side of the house and down the stairs and through the cellar, to the door just as she leaned against it to come through. The bottom board was loose after pressing it close and back against her. I stationed a heavy bar across the cellar door and went back upstairs where the two in the front had disappeared.

Pa stood there and asked, "Where are they?"

I knew if we manned one door they could get back through another.

Who were they? I didn't know. Pa didn't know. We stood there, not moving. Pa with his rifle in hand and me with a board I'd taken from the cellar. The banging started on the back door. I noticed the top latch wasn't pushed across and fastened. The banging stopped. After some time, Pa decided it had been quiet for long enough.

If they were hiding in the cellar, we had not returned back there since I placed the bar across the door, so I didn't care. As long as they couldn't get out.

Pa stepped outside, opened the trapdoor leading to the cellar and climbed inside. I listened for a struggle. Nothing. So I followed him down with my stick in hand and his rifle leading the way. The only thing we heard was our heavy breathing. . I thought maybe I should make sure they don't close us in, so I doubled back to keep anyone from locking the cellar door from the outside. I wished there wasn't a second door so that they couldn't get back in from that part of the cellar connected to the inside of the house. We'd checked the cellar and headed back upstairs, Pa and me, but no one was there, not now. Pa handed the rifle over to me and I led the way out into the wheat field away from the house.

I never looked back, I didn't want to see if someone was standing in the front window watching us walk away. But this time I looked back and turned to the house, lifting the rifle, fired two shots, and the figure and the house disappeared from my view—and my Pa with it. I woke knowing most of that was no dream.

With Henry's uncle and maybe the sheriff on to me, I couldn't stop the nightmares from coming, and they seemed to be getting harder for me to recover from. I knew it was time to get away. I should pack up and head further North . But, I didn't know if I could still face trying to get North without going back home one more time to check on Ma. I knew it was risky, but I had to try.

I didn't go downstairs to play the piano that next afternoon. I'd already packed up the few things I had and gathered what money I'd saved and planned to head for the train station to buy a ticket. In disguise, I'd grown a beard and pulled a black, dusky hat down over my forehead. I looked to be thirty years older than my true age.

I stepped up my plans in the early morning, as Henry sent word to me that he'd tried to hold the law off until the information on Ezra came in from North Carolina, but he was unsuccessful. The sheriff would be here by 10:00 a.m. to arrest me for whatever the man on the train with me had done. It was already 9:30.

Out the window, I saw the sheriff coming to my room 25 minutes early, up the back way, holding handcuffs, ready to haul me to a jail cell. He came alone. Before he arrested me for something I didn't do, I'd fight to get away. Standing behind the door, when he pushed it open, I knocked his gun to the floor, overtook and handcuffed him, then locked him in the room closet. I rushed to grab what things I could, bolted out of my room, and down the back stairway headed straight for the IC depot for the 10:00 train. No one would suspect I had gotten away, since I secured the sheriff in my room closet, and I had seen no bounties posted for me.

Bound for the #4 train to Grenada, which would bypass Hardeman County, I trekked through dense back woods to the Memphis IC depot. I stood on the platform waiting twenty minutes, then looked behind me to see why I felt sure someone had followed and was watching me–hopefully not now.

"Jeremiah?"

There she was, loaded down with two suitcases and wearing a big yellow headscarf. Telma was in an unusual outfit that didn't fit her properly with the skirt slipping down on one side. She stood there hunching it back up to her waist.

"I saw you leave down the stairs from your room," she said.

"What are you doing here and how did you know it was me?"

It was bad enough that she followed me, but she had Caleb with her. Telma was still pulling at that darn skirt before she said anything. I probably shouldn't have con-fided some things and hoped she and her boy didn't be-lieve they were coming with me.

"I will always know you. Don't leave me behind," Telma pleaded.

As the little fella stood holding on to her skirt to keep it from sliding, Telma kept talking.

"I can't take you with me; I don't even know how far I'll get."

I still wasn't sure how much Henry had done to help or hurt me, but what just happened a while ago sure won't do me any good.

"I would be pleasured to go anywhere you go," she said, "no matter what you did or how far you got."

I didn't know what else to say to get her to leave. As we were early and the only ones on this end of the platform, we stood staring at one another until we heard footsteps in the distance coming up far behind her. Telma turned around to look in the direction we'd both just left. Henry had turned the corner and was walking our way.

I believed Telma had brought him along with her to the depot, and it told me that she believed in him more than I did.

"Did you have him follow you here?"

"No, please believe me; I didn't know he was coming."

"But think of everything he tried to do for you, Jeremiah. The least you could do is to say goodbye."

"Why should I? I'm on the run now because he couldn't get me off and I'm going to spend time in jail for something I didn't do."

"Yes, I know all this. But I reckon through all of 'yo disagreements you told me about over injustice, and you running away from somethin', Henry has stood by you, even going against his own folks."

"I guess it wasn't his fault that the guy on the train I met up with had some run-ins with the law. But Henry learned more about me than you or anybody else around here knows and he used it against me."

"I don't think he did. I still don't know all he knows about you, 'cause you never unburdened in fronta' me, but the man that I seen he is– tried to get you off. Either you were to be tried as an unjust Negro's partner or someone whose real name I still don't know– who's hiding from somethin' else."

I thought, at first, I didn't even know Henry was a lawyer. He's so ordinary that way.

"It wasn't until he knew of my trouble and that I might be arrested that he told me his profession. Maybe he should have told me before then," I said.

"Maybe like you, he has his own reasons for keeping parts of his life secret from folks he cares 'bout."

"Okay, maybe you're right, but look Telma, it's like this here, I wanted to at first, but I can't take you and the boy with me now. I'm on the run. It's a long story. My name's really Jake, but I can't talk about it now. You are a good woman and I'll see you again one day. I just can't have nobody with me now, please understand. I hope you do."

Without another word, Telma abruptly picked up her bag, held onto her skirt, and walked off with the boy. I felt terrible, but I didn't know what else I could do.

I'd looked past her walking back and saw that Henry had stopped down at the other end of the platform. He hadn't taken the added steps needed to make it down to where I was standing. He didn't even see us down here, with the other Negro's, I thought. He is not even aware I'm here.

I felt my feet moving in the unsuspecting man's direction. Across the platform, the planks creaked as I crossed over into the White section where he boarded the train, which was 30 minutes late.

With Henry's back towards me, facing the opposite direction, I had to place my hand on his coat sleeve to get him to turn around. Although he hadn't seen me in several weeks– since I told him not to contact me if I had to go the jail– he still knew who I was.

I'm not sure who reached out first, but we embraced with all the emotion of two brothers who knew we'd never meet again.

I never said, a word and neither did he, but we both knew what that moment meant to the other. This was our goodbye, but this time we were separating the way God meant for us to part–as friends.

I walked back to the other end of the platform, but before could get on the train, the jailers spotted me despite my disguise. I did not learn until later that these men, who looked familiar, were not the jailers. Henry, unbeknownst to me, had gotten me off at the last second, just before I escaped from my room. Now, this was someone else after me.

I was a free man—*at least from the law*—but did not know it, as I stood there on the platform with Henry. But Henry knew, and I believe he thought I knew too– before he died. I wish I had known.

******

CH 36

(J)

It was with the utmost sorrow that I took the news that my friend Henry was tragically gone. He died, not trying defend himself, but in defense of every man's right to be free.

I learned of his death when I picked up a copy of *The Colored Citizen* and found that Attorney Henry Lawson had been killed on his way home to Virginia–returning to his family. My faithful friend Henry got off to buy a gift for his wife, the gentleman who sat next to him on the train told the reporter. Henry went out of his way to give his business to a Freedman's store, which was dynamited while he was inside. The explosion also killed the owner, a mother and two children–all hard-working Negros.

After leaving Memphis, I learned Henry came by my place after I'd run off, freed the sheriff and convinced him I—Jake, alias Jeremiah —had done nothing wrong.The arrest warrant out for me was a false one.

Henry had cleared me–his client and friend–who was now to go free. The sheriff, knowing what I was up against, and my fate if they'd caught me let bygones be bygones. I will never forget an earlier conversation we had, which was not long ago, when

Henry finally told me he was a lawyer and would like to defend me.

"We don't get what we earn; we get what people allow us." He'd said.

"So you're saying a little smile and a friendly greeting go a long way."

"With those who have all you want for yourself, it does." Henry added.

Speaking through gritted teeth, I struggled to release my clenched jaw which I had held rigid, imaging myself detained in a filthy, cold jail cell.

"It hasn't worked for me," I told him.

"It did before, if it hadn't, you wouldn't have made this far."

"What about with everybody else, everyday folks?"

"Works with them too," he said,

Henry then motioned to my face, its muscles felt fixed hard and tight across.

"But you've got to try to relax from time to time."

When Henry gave me a final bit of advice that day, I didn't register the faraway look in his eyes. I wonder now, though, if he was saying those last words just for my benefit.

"One more thing," Henry offered, "Sometimes working hard or going away so your folks can be proud of you is not worth it, if you have to take your presence and love from them in the process."

CH 37

(*M*)olly

Struggling up the dirt path, then stopping to stand behind the wide pecan tree, fidgeting with her handbag, was someone I never wanted to see again.

"Here comes Ms. Jackson, Ma. What does she want?" I said, pretending I hadn't seen and overheard that ruckus between them at the Neuman's place.

The woman paraded up to our front door, but surprised when I opened it, twisting herself 'round.

"What do you want here Miss Jean," I called her back.

Ma was standing behind me acting nervous, but I wanted to tell her that there was nothing this woman could say that I didn't already know.

"Wait out here for just one second, Miss Jean" I demanded respectfully as I closed the door in her face.

I took all of thirty seconds to explain to Ma what I already knew about my life, my birth and everything in between. If she was worried about me feeling something bad, she didn't need to worry anymore. I would always love her and was grateful to her and Mr. Neuman for giving me life. That chapter in secrecy was now closed and forever shared by us—in our love for each other. There was nothing we couldn't do together to take down this woman on the other side of the door.

I paced off and opened the door again. Miss Jean was still out there, standing firm. She came right to the point of why she was there.

"Look," Miss Jean blurted out, "Do you know where your brother is?"

"Get away from here." I moved toward her, "My brother is dead and you know it!"

She tried to push past me to get to Ma, but I put out both arms and blocked her way.

"If you go near her again," I said, "I'll hurt you myself 'cause she's too God-fearing to do what I will."

Reaching into her bag, the crazed-eyed woman looked down, then back up at Ma standing behind me. Miss Jean grabbed onto something inside, before releasing it, and slowly slid her hand out— empty.

"I'm so sorry...so, so sorry," she cried, and stumbled backwards away from the door, then fell onto the dirt path. She scrambled up and ran wildly out past the trees and finally disappeared into the open, grassy field.

CH 38

(J)ake

I stopped running. I thought about Henry and Ezra who must have made enough of a difference to make others feel threatened by their very existence. Henry's death, becoming Ezra's momentary acquaintance and almost getting killed and going to jail, all made me realize that not only was I afraid to lose my life, but I was also afraid to live it.

In that moment, I knew my own life was not worth living if I was afraid to defend my own reputation and live the way I wanted to. I read about it, write about it, but I couldn't bring myself to live it so others could see, understand and value my contribution as a man. If I couldn't stand up and fight for my rightful existence, without backing down, then I didn't deserve to live.

After I'd jumped off the train, as it slowed down before the Mississippi state line, I turned around to see how close the three men who were chasing me had gotten. I had had enough of them and anyone else connected with them.

I decided not to take the train all the way to Grenada, so I walked back for a quarter of the distance. I looked past the trees clustered around a small shack illuminated by the early morning sunlight. I knew someone was still after me and wanted me dead, but I didn't see anyone around.

What was that whistling sound?

I heard dogs barking and running... now seeing two black, white and brown bloodhounds in the distance.

"Here...," I said. Thinking that tossing out some smelly meat would distract the hungry, tired dogs away from my scent.

Once off my trail, I backtracked, seeing one of the bounty hunters. That's when I snuck up and grabbed him from behind, knocked him to the ground and took his shotgun.

"You are the same hunters I saw back in Woodall Mountain past Corinth. What is it you want? Tell me, or I'll shoot you dead right here, as I live and breathe."

"Give it over," the man said, lying flat on his back. "We know you're the one with the papers."

Feeling my gun under his throat, he backed off of his demands and then told me everything Lena Neuman had done. He described her part in their gunning down the wrong man for something they thought I had done.

I realized then that they thought Ezra was me. Now they know who I am. I'd mistakenly thought Ezra had committed some menial crime–the reason for him being shot. Then Henry said the law was after him for robbery. But these men thought they we killing me on that mountain because I wouldn't give them something that they wanted. It wouldn't matter if told them I didn't have those papers—the truth.

No more time needed to be wasted listening to this scum or trying get him to listen to the truth.

Up ahead, the shorter and smallest of the men, was roping his horse to an oak tree. While he was separated from the others, I forced him backward with the gun to his head.

Along with the taller man, already secured near the shack between two sturdy magnolias trees, I tied the other culprit using one hand while holding the shot gun in the other.

There was more food still left in my pack. I tossed it to distract another approaching dog howling further ahead. I stopped backtracking and spied the last of the bounty hunters inside the shack in a dead sleep. He looked to be injured, so I kicked in the door and got to his gun lying against the wall. He fell to the floor just trying to get up from the bed. While begging me not to use the gun on him, he pulled a knife out of the back of his trousers. Coming from the left, I felt my fist rise up then pound against his jaw. For some reason, the *Battle Hymn of the Republic* played over and over in my head as my right fist closed in on the other side of his face.

As ye deal with my condemners…
So with you my grace shall deal…
His truth is marching on…

The knife fell to the ground. I pulled up the other shotgun that was resting against my trouser leg, and held both guns on him. I bent down and picked up the knife where he dropped it, and then latched him onto the end of the bed.

With all three hunters, no longer a threat, I headed southeast, towards home, ready to confront Lena and her destructive ways. I knew I could face anyone now and didn't need to go anywhere to prove myself.

I spied Lena through a window, holding up in an abandoned house on the edge of her estate. I had no idea why she'd sent those hunters for me or what papers she was after.

"Lena," I said, dispensing with the Mrs...

Lena flinched when I called through the open window, but did not look out or turn around.

"Did you send out your posse for me? " I hollered.

"Jacob...Jake McCray..." she turned around and walked over to the opening. "You're alive. You're here."

"Open the door," I demanded.

Lena sashayed over and I walked in fuming.

"Don't you dare pull that. You knew I was alive, and you tried to make sure that I didn't stay that way."

I told her I knew she'd sent those men and that I was the one they were to go after the first time at the Hardeman train station, and then hunted into the mountains in Corinth.

"Yes that's true, but I didn't send them for you again after that. I truly thought you had been killed after your own Ma saw your body. I didn't want you dead. I just wanted the deed back, that's all. And I wanted you too," Lena said, grabbing at my arm.

"What do you mean?" I asked.

"I swear, I had no idea you were still alive until they came to me again and asked to be paid. They were suspicious that it wasn't you they'd killed and had an idea where you were. This time, they swore they would get the papers from the right man."

"So if you didn't tell them where to find me, who did?"

"I don't know, but I've got to have those papers you took Jake. Someone like you and your family should never get a piece of my land, not as long as I live. It's just not right."

"Yes, I can tell you're really glad to see me."

"You have no idea." Lena said, stroking the back of my hand.

Lena was the one who had no idea what she was talking about. Her resurfacing haughtiness and overt desire to conquer all things," especially beautiful ones," she'd said, caused her to avert her mission long enough to ask me to succumb to her, once more. Lena and I performed our animalistic tango in the familiar shelter of the shuttered, battered house, with her in the lead.

Although I'd had enough, I pretended to allow her to make me happy as Lena guided me over to an old sofa. This time, though, I was ready to stand my ground.

I had no idea, however; that miles away, at least one of the posse had earlier broken free. He was now arriving on horseback at the outskirts of the Neuman estate. Riding up to the door, he kicked it open. Assuming Lena was being held against her will, he grabbed my shotgun that was lying inside against the plyboard and fired on me. The bullet hit me in the right leg.

Leaving me to die, Lena darted out the door, seemingly to tell her side of the story. What she did not know was another posse member who had escaped also, had been listening outside the open window ten minutes earlier and overheard the *real* struggle between us. But, he was unable or chose not to stop the other one who arrived after him from shooting. Thankfully, it seemed that the younger posse member who arrived first, and who had earlier told me of Lena's plan, had now had enough of the situation. He ventured inside to tie my leg to stop the bleeding and went to get help.

CH 39

(J)

Having your leg in a splint is not so bad. This leg will mend and l may always have a slight limp, but save that– I'll be okay. Lena Neuman is no longer a threat. She no longer will hold her head up so high. One of her own hired men spread the story around town, and to her husband, of her actions with me, the "lowly" mill clerk.

I knew Ma and Molly always behaved like Mr. Neuman was a couple notches below God, but I'm not so sure he really isn't anymore. I wasn't sure he wouldn't want me shot or at least off of his land. But even he thinks less of his wife; not me, it seems. I couldn't believe it when he let me continue as bookkeeper at the mill and even increased my earnings. The increase allowed me to be able to add a room to our place and to pay down on a little store in town with the help of the Freedman's Bureau.

Mr. Neuman's a good man, but I don't expect anything else from him for myself. I want nothing, but what I've earned from him now or ever, although I still plan to move North one day. But, go away to be a man– I know I don't have to anymore.

Since, I still believe Mrs. Neuman was willing to have me killed for those papers, I wanted to know what happened to them.

The day before I left to go North, I had worked at the mill that morning. Mr. Neuman, who was there all day, left around 9 a.m. to take some of the earnings for the week to the bank in town; however, he came back after only 10 minutes. He had forgotten one of the envelopes.

He must have gone into the mill safe, where Mrs. Neuman said she'd left the papers, in an envelope, when she'd stopped in around that time. Mr. Neuman said when he came back and looked for the envelope he'd forgotten, there were two envelopes inside the safe, so he took them, thinking he'd forgotten to take them both with him to the bank. When he got to the bank he handed all three envelopes over to the teller, as he'd already counted out the money earlier at the mill.

By the time the teller noticed that the third envelope Mr. Neuman had given him contained documents instead of currency, Mr. Neuman had already left. The teller placed the envelope containing the personal papers in Mr. Neuman's strong box, but neglected to send word to him that he'd done so.

Lena thought I'd taken those papers, the same ones they later found sitting in an envelope, underneath bonds and other deeds, at the bottom of Mr. Neuman's metal, security box in the bank vault.

One other thing, this last time, when one of Mrs. Neuman's posse said, "Give it over, we know you're the one with the papers," I wondered what papers and how did they know where to find me?

What the man left out when he finally told me Mrs. Neuman was behind everything, was that their posse found me that second time in Memphis–not through Lena, but through Ciaok. They'd gotten hold of the letters I'd given to Ciaok to take to Ma.

It's going to take a long while for me to get over everything that I learned had happened with troubled, tortured Ciaok. He was dead. Either by his own hand or an accident–no one will ever be sure.

He never did come back to give Ma those letters after seeing me in Memphis almost three months ago. I learned later that his body was found with a knife to the stomach. No one was sure if he killed himself. I believe either he did it out of shame or that Lena and her posse had something to do with it. I can't be sure that Ciaok willingly gave the two letters over to those men. If so, then I would have to believe Ciaok and Lena had worked to intercept the very first letter I sent home over a year ago. That was the same letter Ciaok told me Ma never got.

I remember on days when Ciaok would go to the postmaster in Misterton for the Neumans, he'd sometimes pick up mail for Ma to save her the walk. I had sent the letter to her under the name of Jeremiah Grayson on the outer envelope. Ciaok must have known it was a name he'd never seen before, opened it, and learned it was from me. Initially, he must have held on to that letter and never told anyone where I was or that I was alive and in hiding. For some reason, Ciaok did eventually send the first letter to Ma. When… I'm not sure. It could only mean he had a change of heart, at the end. But he never handed her the other letters I gave him in Memphis. I'm sure of it, now.

He may have learned about the land being deeded to Ma and believed it belonged to him. In a perfect world it did, along with all the land around it. Still Ciaok tried to stop those men from coming after me a second time, but he couldn't persuade them, so he killed himself.

Ciaok was found in the deepest wooded area behind Milcreek Pond, slumped beside a tree with a knife in his stomach.

That's where he would go at night to listen to the whippoorwills in the pine-oak woods near the canyon. It's been said their haunting, ethereal singing can sense a soul departing, and can capture it as it flees. I wanted to believe this, and that he had a change of heart and had tried to stop them before it was too late. He was a good man and probably didn't want to live with what he thought he had caused.

I couldn't think about Ciaok now. But, I couldn't get what happened to him out of my mind. I remember one particular conversation we'd had when I'd thought, at the time, that Ciaok had accidently stumbled on me in Memphis disguised as Jeremiah.

"Folks always pretending you're invisible, if they can," Ciaok had said, "if you say nothing… if you let them."

"You know why?" He went on, "cause that's what they want you to be."

In his soul, poor Ciaok was tormented every moment of his life by the betrayal of those his people had trusted. How could he do anything but what he did?

I believe Ciaok wanted to make amends for taking the first letter that he used to find me, but it was too late. Lena and her posse got wind of it. They found out where I was from him.

In the end, the final two letters that I gave Ciaok were discovered locked in Lena's personal chest. Although Lena said she only wanted the deed back, the woman wanted me dead and was going to have me finished off. I knew that she was behind Ciaok's death in some way.

Before falling off to sleep from exhaustion, my last thought was something I'd said to Ciaok just before he left Memphis.

"Even though the world has kicked you in the teeth, my friend, I believe you can still find some kind of happiness."

CH 40

Jake

Fully aware that Lena Neuman was ruthless, and had always gotten her way, I knew the battle was not over. I caught up with her after the doctors stitched me up and handed me a wooden crutch to get around.

I hobbled over, stepping right up to the white columned estate. Lena Neuman looked shocked when she opened the front door of her two-story manor house to see me standing there ready to finish what I should have a long time ago.

"I'll tell you this just once." I said. "Papers or no papers, I'm gonna stay right here, petition to buy some land and use the earnings from the mill—if your good husband will still have me —to open a store."

She looked at me with cold eyes and no expression on her face.

"Uh… oh," she mumbled, turning around to see if anyone was behind her listening.

"Either way," I said, "I'm not going to allow someone like you to make me your 'boy' to be at your beck and call, doing things I'm ashamed of with you; a married woman. Yes, I know your ways; you think I'll fall every time, but I didn't and I won't. Never again, not anymore."

CH 41

Molly

Now tired, I walked back in the house after a long walk to the Freedman's store early that morning. I'd been thinking about the letter that came from Henry Lawson, Attorney at Law, dated two weeks ago. That's how Ma and I learned that Jake was still alive, having worked in a saloon in Memphis, and may be in jail somewhere. We didn't know where to go to find him, though, as he was no longer where the letter stated he had been, according the response from the wire Mr. Neuman sent.

That joy Ma talked about was waning for me as we tried to find where Jake was and how we could get to him.

"Ma, I'm back." I said, walking in the door expecting and hoping Ma would still be like her old self and not reverting to the other person–because of the waiting. I took off my shoes as Ma had just mopped the floor before I left.

"Ouch!" I yelled.

Ma turned around, "What's wrong?"

"I stepped on something," I said. "I know I just swept this floor only a few hours ago and didn't you just mop?"

"Uh-huh." She said.

"Well…what's that I just stepped on? What are you smiling like that for?"

I bent down to pick up the sharp object from the floor.

"What's this?"

I'd gathered up two small half shells lying in the middle of the living room floor. Ma didn't eat pecans and I didn't have any before I left that morning. But here they were- brown husks, pecan shells. I jerked right up, stumbling over my own feet as I ran towards the back room, screaming.

I could see my brother and me, together again, our faces to the sky, his lunchbox filled with messy pecan shells and me crying—"Stankin',stankin' squirrel, stinkin'…."—over and over again.

On a crutch, Jake hobbled out of the back room, past Ma's beaming face. He was dressed in the speckled, yellow shirt and grey-stitched trousers he'd packed that day. I felt myself falling to the floor, but he grabbed me and held me up against him and his crutch.

"Yes, Molly, it's me," Jake said, with a wide grin and tears in his eyes. "Your stinkin' squirrel."

The three of us—Ma, Jake and me grabbed one another. Our tears poured freely. We took turns dabbing each other's eyes with a handkerchief.

Then Jake explained where he'd been and what had happened, while we all fell down-still holding on to one another on the long worn sofa. We were ecstatic and exhausted from the best day of our lives.

But what he said next shot Ma and me right out of our seats and out of our euphoric peace.

"I'll be here with you for, oh, 'bout two months just to heal up," Jake said, "but then, I have to leave again."

Ma just about slapped him.

"Oh, Lord no. Mercy. Please. You're not going away again," Ma cried as she pulled on his crutch to keep him from going off.

"Not for long, I'll be back," Jake grinned. "You both can come with me if you want. I have someone I want you to meet."

Wrapped together, the three of us stepped through the front doorway and out into the sunshine, peering up into the clear blue sky where Woodall Mountain, Hardeman County, and even Boston were a distant, shuttered memory.

Through tears of joy, I now understood Jake's writing: You, me, family, everyone enclosed....still seeing, yet believing...forever.

****

About The Author

Kay Carroll leads a busy life teaching high schoolers about the history of the United States along with strategies to prepare them for life's challenges. She lives with her husband and son in the Chicagoland area.

References in order of appearance:

http://alabamamaps.ua.edu/historicalmaps/us_states/mississippi/

http://www.davidwalkermemorial.org/black-boston

https://www.google.com/search?q=The+Baptist+Sentienalcha&oq=The+Baptist+Sentien-alcha&aqs=chrome..69i57.2096949j0j4&sourceid=chrome&ie=UTF-8

(http://www.south-end-boston.com/History)

http://americasbesthistory.com/abhtimeline1860.html)

(http://www.nlm.nih.gov/changingthefaceofmedicine/physicians/biography_35.html

http://en.wikipedia.org/wiki/Smithsonian_Institution)　　http://americasbesthistory.com/abhtimeline1820.html).

Prologue(citation:http://americasbesthis-tory.com/abhtimeline1860.html)

http://en.wikipedia.org/wiki/Smithsonian_Institution) http://americasbesthistory.com/abhtimeline1820.html).

h2ttp://phrontistery.info/archaic.html

http://mess1.homestead.com/nineteenth_century_slang_dictionary.pdf

http://www.legendsofamerica.com/we-slang-b.html

The Black Press in Mississippi, 1865- 1895

https://books.google.com/books?id=fQ4JiuThqfAC&pg=PA8&lpg=PA8&dq=black+publications+from+1880%27s&source=bl&ots=OouK-McUYX&sig=P7aPWRk9M-Pf9T4hUi5WZvBGno8&hl=en&sa=X&ved=0ahUKEwjYyY_J-NLKAhVM4mMKHeFVAWMQ6AEIKzAC#v=onep

age&q=black%20publica-tions%20from%201880's&f=false

University of Mississippi Libraries http://www.ole-miss.edu/depts/general_library/archives/find-ing_aids/MUM00181.html#ref455

University Library

University of Illinois at Urbana-Cham-paignhttp://www.library.illinois.edu/hpnl/newspa-pers/historical.php

Gale: U.S History in Context Everyday life: Fashion http://ic.galegroup.com/ic/uhic/ReferenceDetail-sPage/ReferenceDetailsWin-dow?zid=f60e5de82d2a8166e6f8f5f95a273f3b&ac-tion=2&catId=&documen-tId=GALE%7CCX2536601691&userGroup-Name=oldt1017&jsid=1e67e95acab586e5cf93b2e370b22ea1

Elizabeth Blackwell
(http://www.nlm.nih.gov/changingthefaceofmedicine/physicians/biography_35.html

(Meals   of the south) http://www.foodbycountry.com/Spain-to-Zimbabwe-Cumulative-Index/United-States-Southern-Region.html

(http://www.south-end-boston.com/History)

Made in the USA
Coppell, TX
05 August 2021

59990825R00146